# MASTERS OF THE MACABRE

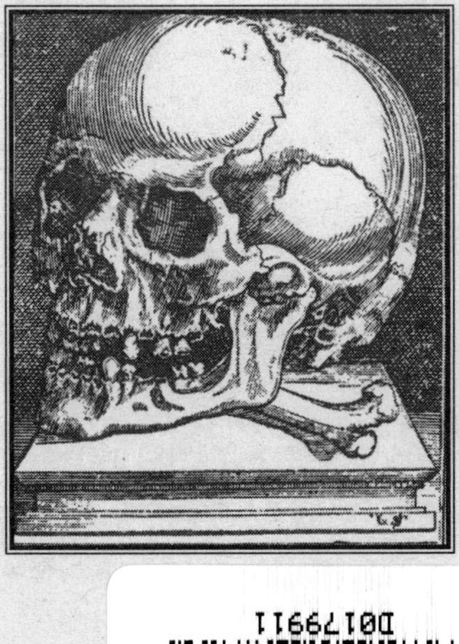



Book-of-the-Month Club
New York

Michael O'Mara Books Limited
9 Lion Yard
Tremadoc Road
London SW4 7NQ

Designed and Typeset by The Florence Group, Stoodleigh, Devon, UK

Printed and bound by Cox & Wyman, Reading, UK

# Contents

# The Adventure of the German Student

*Washington Irving*

On a stormy night in the tempestuous times of the French revolution, a young German was returning to his lodgings, at a late hour, across the old part of Paris. The lightning gleamed, and the loud claps of thunder rattled through the lofty narrow streets—but I should now tell you something about this young German.

Gottfried Wolfgang was a young man of good family. He had studied for some time at Göttingen, but being of a visionary and enthusiastic character, he had wandered into those wild and speculative doctrines which have so often bewildered German students. His secluded life, his intense application, and the singular nature of his studies, had an effect on both mind and body. His health was impaired, his imagination diseased. He had been indulging in fanciful speculations on spiritual essences, until, like Swedenborg, he had an ideal world of his own around him. He took up a notion, I do not know from what cause, that there was an evil influence hanging over him; an evil genius or spirit seeking to ensnare him and ensure his perdition. Such an idea working on his melancholy temperament, produced the most gloomy effects. He became haggard and desponding. His friends discovered the mental malady preying upon him, and determined that the best cure was a change of scene; he was sent, therefore, to finish his studies amidst the splendors and gayeties of Paris.

Wolfgang arrived at Paris at the breaking out of the revolution. The popular delirium at first caught his enthusiastic mind, and he was captivated by the political and philosophical theories of the day: but the scenes of blood which followed shocked his sensitive nature, disgusted him with society and the world, and made him more than ever a recluse. He shut himself up in a solitary apartment in the *Pays*

*Latin*, the quarter of the students. There, in a gloomy street not far from the monastic walls of the Sorbonne, he pursued his favorite speculations. Sometimes he spent hours together in the great libraries of Paris, those catacombs of departed authors, rummaging among their hordes of dusty and obsolete works in quest of food for his unhealthy appetite. He was, in a manner, a literary ghoul, feeding in the charnel-house of decayed literature.

Wolfgang, though solitary and reclusive, was of an ardent temperament, but for a time it operated merely upon his imagination. He was too shy and ignorant of the world to make any advances to the fair, but he was a passionate admirer of female beauty, and in his lonely chamber would often lose himself in reveries on forms and faces which he had seen, and his fancy would deck out images of loveliness far surpassing the reality.

While his mind was in this excited and sublimated state, a dream produced an extraordinary effect upon him. It was of a female face of transcendent beauty. So strong was the impression made, that he dreamt of it again and again. It haunted his thoughts by day, his slumbers by night; in fine, he became passionately enamoured of this shadow of a dream. This lasted so long that it became one of those fixed ideas which haunt the minds of melancholy men, and are at times mistaken for madness.

Such was Gottfried Wolfgang, and such his situation at the time I mentioned. He was returning home late one stormy night, through some of the old and gloomy streets of the *Marais*, the ancient part of Paris. The loud claps of thunder rattled among the high houses of the narrow streets. He came to the Place de Grêve, the square where public executions are performed. The lightning quivered about the pinnacles of the ancient Hôtel de Ville, and shed flickering gleams over the open space in front. As Wolfgang was crossing the square, he shrank back with horror at finding himself close by the guillotine. It was the height of the reign of terror, when this dreadful instrument of death stood ever ready, and its scaffold was continually running with the blood of the virtuous and the brave. It had that very day been actively employed in the work of carnage, and there it stood in grim array, amidst a silent and sleeping city, waiting for fresh victims.

Wolfgang's heart sickened within him, and he was turning shuddering from the horrible engine, when he beheld a shadowy form, cowering as it were at the foot of the steps which led up to the scaffold. A succession of vivid flashes of lightning revealed it more distinctly. It was a female figure, dressed in black. She was seated on one of the lower steps of the scaffold, leaning forward, her face hid in her lap; and her long dishevelled tresses hanging to the ground, streaming with the rain which fell in torrents. Wolfgang paused. There was something awful in this solitary monument of woe. The female had the appearance of being above the common order. He knew the times to be full of vicissitude, and that many a fair head, which had once been pillowed on down, now wandered houseless. Perhaps this was some poor mourner whom the dreadful axe had rendered desolate, and who sat here heart-broken on the strand of existence, from which all that was dear to her had been launched into eternity.

He approached, and addressed her in the accents of sympathy. She raised her head and gazed wildly at him. What was his astonishment at beholding, by the bright glare of the lightning, the very face which had haunted him in his dreams. It was pale and disconsolate, but ravishingly beautiful.

Trembling with violent and conflicting emotions, Wolfgang again accosted her. He spoke something of her being exposed at such an hour of the night, and to the fury of such a storm, and offered to conduct her to her friends. She pointed to the guillotine with a gesture of dreadful signification.

"I have no friend on earth!" she said.

"But you have a home," said Wolfgang.

"Yes—in the grave!"

The heart of the student melted at the words.

"If a stranger dare make an offer," said he, "without danger of being misunderstood, I would offer my humble dwelling as a shelter; myself as a devoted friend. I am friendless myself in Paris, and a stranger in the land; but if my life could be of service, it is at your disposal, and should be sacrificed before harm or indignity should come to you."

There was an honest earnestness in the young man's manner that had its effect. His foreign accent, too, was in his favor; it showed him not to be a hackneyed inhabitant of Paris. Indeed, there is an eloquence in true enthusiasm that is not to be doubted. The homeless stranger confided herself implicitly to the protection of the student.

He supported her faltering steps across the Pont Neuf, and by the place where the statue of Henry the Fourth had been overthrown by the populace. The storm had abated, and the thunder rumbled at a distance. All Paris was quiet; that great volcano of human passion slumbered for a while, to gather fresh strength for the next day's eruption. The student conducted his charge through the ancient streets of the *Pays Latin*, and by the dusky walls of the Sorbonne, to the great dingy hotel which he inhabited. The old portress who admitted them stared with surprise at the unusual sight of the melancholy Wolfgang with a female companion.

On entering his apartment, the student, for the first time, blushed at the scantiness and indifference of his dwelling. He had but one chamber—an old-fashioned saloon—heavily carved, and fantastically furnished with the remains of former magnificence, for it was one of those hotels in the quarter of the Luxembourg palace, which had once belonged to nobility. It was lumbered with books and papers, and all the usual apparatus of a student, and his bed stood in a recess at one end.

When lights were brought, and Wolfgang had a better opportunity of contemplating the stranger, he was more than ever intoxicated by her beauty. Her face was pale, but of a dazzling fairness, set off by a profusion of raven hair that hung clustering about it. Her eyes were large and brilliant, with a singular expression approaching almost to wildness. As far as her black dress permitted her shape to be seen, it was of perfect symmetry. Her whole appearance was highly striking, though she was dressed in the simplest style. The only thing approaching to an ornament which she wore, was a broad black band round her neck, clasped by diamonds.

The perplexity now commenced with the student how to dispose of the helpless being thus thrown upon his protection. He thought

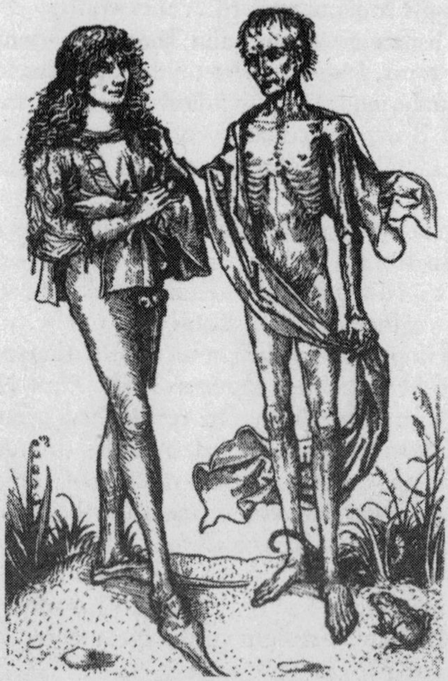

of abandoning his chamber to her, and seeking shelter for himself elsewhere. Still he was so fascinated by her charms, there seemed to be such a spell upon his thoughts and senses, that he could not tear himself from her presence. Her manner, too, was singular and unaccountable. She spoke no more of the guillotine. Her grief had abated. The attentions of the student had first won her confidence, and then, apparently, her heart. She was evidently an enthusiast like himself, and enthusiasts soon understand each other.

In the infatuation of the moment, Wolfgang avowed his passion for her. He told her the story of his mysterious dream, and how she had possessed his heart before he had even seen her. She was strangely affected by his recital, and acknowledged to have felt an impulse towards him equally unaccountable. It was the time for wild theory and wild actions. Old prejudices and superstitions were done away; everything was under the sway of the "Goddess of Reason." Among other rubbish of the old times, the forms and ceremonies of marriage began to be considered superfluous bonds for honorable minds. Social compacts were the vogue. Wolfgang was too much of a theorist not to be tainted by the liberal doctrines of the day.

"Why should we separate?" said he; "our hearts are united; in the eye of reason and honor we are as one. What need is there of sordid forms to bind high souls together?"

The stranger listened with emotion: she had evidently received illumination at the same school.

"You have no home or family," continued he, "let me be everything to you, or rather let us be everything to one another. If form is necessary, form shall be observed—there is my hand. I pledge myself to you forever."

"Forever?" said the stranger, solemnly.

"Forever!" repeated Wolfgang.

The stranger clasped the hand extended to her: "Then I am yours," murmured she, and sank upon his bosom.

The next morning the student left his bride sleeping, and sallied forth at an early hour to seek more spacious apartments suitable to the change in his situation. When he returned, he found the stranger lying with her head hanging over the bed, and one arm thrown over it. He spoke to her, but received no reply. He advanced to awaken her from her uneasy posture. On taking her hand, it was cold—there was no pulsation—her face was pallid and ghastly. In a word, she was a corpse.

Horrified and frantic, he alarmed the house. A scene of confusion ensued. The police was summoned. As the officer of police entered the room, he started back on beholding the corpse.

"Great heaven!" cried he, "how did this woman come here?"

"Do you know anything about her?" said Wolfgang eagerly.

"Do I?" exclaimed the officer: "she was guillotined yesterday."

He stepped forward; undid the black collar around the neck of the corpse, and the head rolled on the floor!

The student burst into a frenzy. "The fiend! the fiend has gained possession of me!" shrieked he; "I am lost forever."

They tried to soothe him, but in vain. He was possessed with the frightful belief that an evil spirit had reanimated the dead body to ensnare him. He went distracted, and died in a mad-house.

Here the old gentleman with the haunted head finished his narrative.

"And is this really a fact?" said the inquisitive gentleman.

"A fact not to be doubted," replied the other. "I had it from the best authority. The student told it me himself. I saw him in a mad-house in Paris."

# THE COBWEB

*Saki*

The farmhouse kitchen probably stood where it did as a matter of accident or haphazard choice; yet its situation might have been planned by a master-strategist in farmhouse architecture. Dairy and poultry-yard, and herb garden, and all the busy places of the farm seemed to lead by easy access into its wide flagged haven, where there was room for everything and where muddy boots left traces that were easily swept away. And yet, for all that it stood so well in the centre of human bustle, its long, latticed window, with the wide window-seat, built into an embrasure beyond the huge fireplace, looked out on a wild spreading view of hill and heather and wooded combe. The window nook made almost a little room in itself, quite the pleasantest room in the farm as far as situation and capabilities went. Young Mrs. Ladbruk, whose husband had just come into the farm by way of inheritance, cast covetous eyes on this snug corner, and her fingers itched to make it bright and cozy with chintz curtains and bowls of flowers, and a shelf or two of old china. The musty farm parlour, looking out to a prim, cheerless garden imprisoned within high, blank walls, was not a room that lent itself readily either to comfort or decoration.

"When we are more settled I shall work wonders in the way of making the kitchen habitable," said the young woman to her occasional visitors. There was an unspoken wish in those words, a wish which was unconfessed as well as unspoken. Emma Ladbruk was the mistress of the farm; jointly with her husband she might have her say, and to a certain extent her way, in ordering its affairs. But she was not mistress of the kitchen.

On one of the shelves of an old dresser, in company with chipped sauce-boats, pewter jugs, cheese-graters, and paid bills, rested a worn and ragged Bible, on whose front page was the record, in faded ink, of a baptism dated ninety-four years ago. "Martha Crale" was the name written on that yellow page. The yellow, wrinkled old dame

who hobbled and muttered about the kitchen, looking like a dead autumn leaf which the winter winds still pushed hither and thither, had once been Martha Crale; for seventy odd years she had been Martha Mountjoy. For longer than any one could remember she had pattered to and fro between oven and wash-house and dairy, and out to chicken-run and garden, grumbling and muttering and scolding, but working unceasingly. Emma Ladbruk, of whose coming she took as little notice as she would of a bee wandering in at a window on a summer's day, used at first to watch her with a kind of frightened curiosity. She was so old and so much a part of the place, it was difficult to think of her exactly as a living thing. Old Shep, the white-nozzled, stiff-limbed collie, waiting for his time to die, seemed almost more human than the withered, dried-up old woman. He had been a riotous, roystering puppy, mad with the joy of life, when she was already a tottering, hobbling dame; now he was just a blind, breathing carcase, nothing more, and she still worked with frail energy, still swept and baked and washed, fetched and carried. If there were something in these wise old dogs that did not perish utterly with death, Emma used to think to herself, what generations of ghost-dogs there must be out on those hills, that Martha had reared and fed and tended and spoken a last good-bye word to in that old kitchen. And what memories she must have of human generations that had passed away in her time. It was difficult for any one, let alone a stranger like Emma, to get her to talk of the days that had been; her shrill, quavering speech was of doors that had been left unfastened, pails that had got mislaid, calves whose feeding-time was overdue, and the various little faults and lapses that chequer a farmhouse routine. Now and again, when election time came round, she would unstore her recollections of the old names round which the fight had waged in the days gone by. There had been a Palmerston, that had been a name down Tiverton way; Tiverton was not a far journey as the crow flies, but to Martha it was almost a foreign country. Later there had been Northcotes and Aclands, and many other newer names that she had forgotten; the names changed, but it was always Libruls and Toories, Yellows and Blues. And they always quarrelled and shouted as to who was right and who was wrong. The one they quarrelled about most was a fine old gentleman with an angry face—she had seen his picture on the walls. She had seen it on the floor too, with a rotten apple squashed over it, for the farm had changed its politics from time to time. Martha had never been on one side or the other; none of "they" had ever done the farm a stroke of good. Such was her sweeping verdict, given with all a peasant's distrust of the outside world.

When the half-frightened curiosity had somewhat faded away, Emma Ladbruk was uncomfortably conscious of another feeling towards the old woman. She was a quaint old tradition, lingering about the place, she was part and parcel of the farm itself, she was something at once pathetic and picturesque—but she was dreadfully in the way. Emma had come to the farm full of plans for little reforms and improvements, in part the result of training in the newest ways and methods, in part the outcome of her own ideas and fancies. Reforms in the kitchen region, if those deaf ears could have been induced to give them even a hearing, would have met with short shrift and scornful rejection, and the kitchen region spread over the zone of dairy and market business and half the work of the household. Emma, with the latest science of dead-poultry dressing at her fingertips, sat by, an unheeded watcher, while old Martha trussed the chickens for the market-stall as she had trussed them for nearly fourscore years—all leg and no breast. And the hundred hints anent effective cleaning and labour-lightening and the things that make for wholesomeness which the young woman was ready to impart or to put into action dropped away into nothingness before that wan, muttering, unheeding presence. Above all, the coveted window corner, that was to be a dainty, cheerful oasis in the gaunt old kitchen, stood now choked and lumbered with a litter of odds and ends that Emma, for all her nominal authority, would not have dared or cared to displace; over them seemed to be spun the protection of something that was like a human cobweb. Decidedly Martha was in the way. It would have been an unworthy meanness to have wished to see the span of that brave old life shortened by a few paltry months, but as the days sped by Emma was conscious that the wish was there, disowned though it might be, lurking at the back of her mind.

She felt the meanness of the wish come over her with a qualm of self-reproach one day when she came into the kitchen and found an unaccustomed state of things in that usually busy quarter. Old Martha was not working. A basket of corn was on the floor by her side, and out in the yard the poultry were beginning to clamour a protest of overdue feeding-time. But Martha sat huddled in a shrunken bunch on the window seat, looking out with her dim old eyes as though she saw something stranger than the autumn landscape.

"Is anything the matter, Martha?" asked the young woman.

"'Tis death, 'tis death a-coming," answered the quavering voice; "I knew 'twere coming. I knew it. 'Tweren't for nothing that old Shep's been howling all morning. An' last night I heard the screech-owl give the death-cry, and there were something white as run across the yard yesterday; 'tweren't a cat nor a stoat, 'twere something. The fowls knew 'twere something; they all drew off to one side. Ay, there's been warnings. I knew it were a-coming."

The young woman's eyes clouded with pity. The old thing sitting there so white and shrunken had once been a merry, noisy child, playing about in lanes and hay-lofts and farmhouse garrets; that had been eighty odd years ago, and now she was just a frail old body cowering under the approaching chill of the death that was coming at last to take her. It was not probable that much could be done for her, but Emma hastened away to get assistance and counsel. Her husband, she knew, was down at a tree-felling some little distance off, but she might find some other intelligent soul who knew the old woman better than she did. The farm, she soon found out, had that faculty common to farmyards of swallowing up and losing its human population. The poultry followed her in interested fashion, and swine grunted interrogations at her from behind the bars of their sties, but barnyard and rickyard, orchard and stables and dairy, gave no reward to her search. Then, as she retraced her steps towards the kitchen, she came suddenly on her cousin, young Mr. Jim, as every one called him, who divided his time between amateur horse-dealing, rabbit-shooting, and flirting with the farm maids.

"I'm afraid old Martha is dying," said Emma. Jim was not the sort of person to whom one had to break news gently.

"Nonsense," he said; "Martha means to live to a hundred. She told me so, and she'll do it."

"She may be actually dying at this moment, or it may just be the beginning of the break-up," persisted Emma, with a feeling of contempt for the slowness and dulness of the young man.

A grin spread over his good-natured features.

"It don't look like it," he said, nodding towards the yard. Emma turned to catch the meaning of his remark. Old Martha stood in the middle of a mob of poultry scattering handfuls of grain around her. The turkey-cock, with the bronzed sheen of his feathers and the purple-red of his wattles, the game-cock with the flowing metallic lustre of his Eastern plumage, the hens, with their ochres and buffs and umbers and their scarlet combs, and the drakes, with their bottle-green heads, made a medley of rich colour, in the centre of which the old woman looked like a withered stalk standing amid the riotous growth of gaily-hued flowers. But she threw the grain deftly amid the wilderness of beaks, and her quavering voice carried as far as the two people who were watching her. She was still harping on the theme of death coming to the farm.

"I knew 'twere a-coming. There's been signs an' warnings."

"Who's dead, then, old Mother?" called out the young man.

"'Tis young Mister Ladbruk," she shrilled back; "they've just a-carried his body in. Run out of the way of a tree that was coming down an' ran hisself on to an iron post. Dead when they picked un up. Ay, I knew 'twere coming."

And she turned to fling a handful of barley at a belated group of guinea-fowl that came racing toward her.

The farm was a family property, and passed to the rabbit-shooting cousin as the next-of-kin. Emma Ladbruk drifted out of its history as a bee that had wandered in at an open window might flit its way out again. On a cold grey morning she stood waiting with her boxes already stowed in the farm cart, till the last of the market produce should be ready, for the train she was to catch was of less importance than the chickens and butter and eggs that were to be offered for sale. From where she stood she could see an angle of the long latticed window that was to have been cozy with curtains and gay with bowls of flowers. Into her mind came the thought that for months, perhaps for years, long after she had been utterly forgotten, a white, unheeding face would be seen peering out through those latticed panes, and a weak muttering voice would be heard quavering up and down those flagged passages. She made her way to a narrow barred casement that opened into the farm larder. Old Martha was standing at a table trussing a pair of chickens for the market stall as she had trussed them for nearly fourscore years.

# The Signal-Man

*Charles Dickens*

"Halloa! Below there!"

When he heard a voice thus calling to him, he was standing at the door of his box, with a flag in his hand, furled round its short pole. One would have thought, considering the nature of the ground, that he could not have doubted from what quarter the voice came; but, instead of looking up to where I stood on the top of the steep cutting nearly over his head, he turned himself about and looked down the Line. There was something remarkable in his manner of doing so, though I could not have said, for my life, what. But, I know it was remarkable enough to attract my notice, even though his figure was foreshortened and shadowed, down in the deep trench, and mine was high above him, so steeped in the flow of an angry sunset that I had shaded my eyes with my hand before I saw him at all.

"Halloa! Below!"

From looking down the Line, he turned himself about again, and, raising his eyes, saw my figure high above him.

"Is there any path by which I can come down and speak to you?"

He looked up at me without replying, and I looked down at him without pressing him too soon with a repetition of my idle question. Just then, there came a vague vibration in the earth and air, quickly changing into a violent pulsation, and an oncoming rush that caused me to start back, as though it had force to draw me down. When such vapour as rose to my height from this rapid train had passed me and was skimming away over the landscape, I looked down again, and saw him re-furling the flag he had shown while the train went by.

I repeated my enquiry. After a pause, during which he seemed to regard me with fixed attention, he motioned with his rolled-up flag towards a point on my level some two or three hundred yards distant. I called down to him, "All right!" and made for that point. There, by dint of looking closely about me, I found a rough zigzag descending path notched out: which I followed.

The cutting was extremely deep, and unusually precipitate. It was made through a clammy stone that became oozier and wetter as I went down. For these reasons, I found the way long enough to give me time to recall a singular air of reluctance or compulsion with which he had pointed out the path.

When I came down low enough upon the zigzag descent, to see him again, I saw that he was standing between the rails on the way by which the train had lately passed, in an attitude as if he were waiting for me to appear. He had his left hand at his chin, and that left elbow rested on his right hand crossed over his breast. His attitude was one of such expectation and watchfulness, that I stopped a moment, wondering at it.

I resumed my downward way, and, stepping out upon the level of the railroad and drawing nearer to him, saw that he was a dark sallow man, with a dark beard and rather heavy eyebrows. His post was in as solitary and dismal a place as ever I saw. On either side, a dripping wet wall of jagged stone, excluding all view but a strip of sky; the perspective one way, only a crooked prolongation of this great dungeon; the shorter perspective in the other direction, terminating in a gloomy red light, and the gloomier entrance to a black tunnel, in whose massive architecture there was a barbarous, depressing and

forbidding air. So little sunlight ever found its way to this spot, that it had an earthy, deadly smell; and so much cold wind rushed through it, that it struck chill to me, as if I had left the natural world.

Before he stirred, I was near enough to him to have touched him. Not even then removing his eyes from mine, he stepped back one step, and lifted his hand.

This was a lonesome post to occupy (I said), and it had riveted my attention when I looked down from up yonder. A visitor was a rarity, I should suppose; not an unwelcome rarity, I hoped? In me, he merely saw a man who had been shut up within narrow limits all his life, and who, being at last set free, had a newly awakened interest in these great works. To such purpose I spoke to him; but I am far from sure of the terms I used, for, besides that I am not happy in opening any conversation, there was something in the man that daunted me.

He directed a most curious look towards the red light near the tunnel's mouth, and looked all about it, as if something were missing from it, and then looked at me.

That light was part of his charge? Was it not?

He answered in a low voice: "Don't you know it is?"

The monstrous thought came into my mind as I perused the fixed eyes and the saturnine face, that this was a spirit, not a man. I have speculated since, whether there may have been an infection in his mind.

In my turn, I stepped back. But in making the action, I detected in his eyes some latent fear of me. This put the monstrous thought to flight.

"You look at me," I said, forcing a smile, "as if you had a dread of me."

"I was doubtful," he returned, "whether I had seen you before."

"Where?"

He pointed to the red light he had looked at.

"There?" I said.

Intently watchful of me, he replied (but without sound), "Yes."

"My good fellow, what should I do there? However, be that as it may, I never was there, you may swear."

"I think I may," he rejoined. "Yes. I am sure I may."

His manner cleared, like my own. He replied to my remarks with readiness, and in well chosen words. Had he much to do there? Yes; that was to say, he had enough responsibility to bear; but exactness and watchfulness were what was required of him, and of actual work—manual labour he had next to none. To change that signal, to trim those lights, and to turn this iron handle now and then, was all he had to do under that head. Regarding those many long and lonely hours of which I seemed to make so much, he could only say that the routine of his life had shaped itself into that form, and he had grown used to it. He had taught himself a language down here—if only to know it by sight, and to have formed his own crude ideas of its pronunciation, could be called learning it. He had also worked at fractions and decimals, and tried a little algebra; but he was, and had been as a boy, a poor hand at figures. Was it necessary for him when on duty, always to remain in that channel of damp air, and could he never rise into the sunshine from between those high stone walls? Why, that depended upon times and circumstances. Under some conditions there would be less upon the Line than under others, and the same held good as to certain hours of the day and night. In bright weather, he did choose occasions for getting a little above these lower shadows; but, being at all times liable to be called by his electric bell, and at such times listening for it with redoubled anxiety, the relief was less than I would suppose.

He took me into his box, where there was a fire, a desk for an official book in which he had to make certain entries, a telegraphic instrument with its dial face and needles, and the little bell of which he had spoken. On my trusting that he would excuse the remark that he had been well educated, and (I hoped I might say without offence), perhaps educated above that station, he observed that instances of slight incongruity in such-wise would rarely be found wanting among large bodies of men; that he had heard it was so in workhouses, in the police force, even in that last desperate resource, the army; and that he knew it was so, more or less, in any great railway staff. He had been, when young (if I could believe it, sitting in that hut; he scarcely could), a student of natural philosophy, and had attended lectures; but he had run wild, misused his opportunities, gone down, and never risen again. He had no complaint to offer about that. He had made his bed, and he lay upon it. It was far too late to make another.

All that I have here condensed, he said in a quiet manner, with his grave dark regards divided between me and the fire. He threw in the word "Sir" from time to time, and especially when he referred to his youth: as though to request me to understand that he claimed to be nothing but what I found him. He was several times interrupted by the little bell, and had to read off messages, and send replies. Once, he had to stand without the door, and display a flag as a train passed, and make some verbal communication to the driver. In the discharge of his duties, I observed him to be remarkably exact and vigilant, breaking off his discourse at a syllable, and remaining silent until what he had to do was done.

In a word, I should have set this man down as one of the safest of men to be employed in that capacity, but for the circumstance that while he was speaking to me he twice broke off with a fallen colour, turned his face towards the little bell when it did *not* ring, opened the door of the hut (which was kept shut to exclude the unhealthy damp), and looked towards the red light near the mouth of the tunnel. On both those occasions, he came back to the fire with the inexplicable air upon him which I had remarked, without being able to define, when we were so far asunder.

Said I when I rose to leave him: "You almost make me think that I have met with a contented man."

(I am afraid I must acknowledge that I said it to lead him on.)

"I believe I used to be so," he rejoined, in the low voice in which he had first spoken; "but I am troubled, sir, I am troubled."

He would have recalled the words if he could. He had said them, however, and I took them up quickly.

"With what? What is your trouble?"

"It is very difficult to impart, sir. It is very, very difficult to speak of. If ever you make me another visit, I will try to tell you."

"But I expressly intend to make you another visit. Say, when shall it be?"

"I go off early in the morning, and I shall be on again at ten tomorrow night, sir."

"I will come at eleven."

He thanked me, and went out at the door with me. "I'll show my white light, sir," he said, in his peculiar low voice, "till you have found the way up. When you have found it, don't call out! And when you are at the top, don't call out!"

His manner seemed to make the place strike colder to me, but I said no more than "Very well."

"And when you come down tomorrow night, don't call out! Let me ask you a parting question. What made you cry 'Halloa! Below there!' tonight?"

"Heaven knows," said I. "I cried something to that effect——"

"Not to that effect, sir. Those were the very words. I know them well."

"Admit those were the very words. I said them, no doubt, because I saw you below."

"For no other reason?"

"What other reason could I possibly have?"

"You had no feeling that they were conveyed to you in any supernatural way?"

"No."

He wished me goodnight, and held up his light. I walked by the side of the down Line of rails (with a very disagreeable sensation of a train coming behind me), until I found the path. It was easier to mount than to descend, and I got back to my inn without any adventure.

Punctual to my appointment, I placed my foot on the first notch of the zigzag next night, as the distant clocks were striking eleven. He was waiting for me at the bottom, with his white light on. "I have not called out," I said, when we came close together; "may I speak now?" "By all means, sir." "Goodnight then, and here's my hand." "Goodnight, sir, and here's mine." With that, we walked side by side to his box, entered it, closed the door, and sat down by the fire.

"I have made up my mind, sir," he began, bending forward as soon as we were seated, and speaking in a tone but a little above a whisper, "that you shall not have to ask me twice what troubles me. I took you for someone else yesterday evening. That troubles me."

"That mistake?"

"No. That someone else."

"Who is it?"

"I don't know."

"Like me?"

"I don't know. I never saw the face. The left arm is across the face, and the right arm is waved. Violently waved. This way."

I followed his action with my eyes, and it was the action of an arm gesticulating with the utmost passion and vehemence: "For God's sake clear the way!"

"One moonlit night," said the man, "I was sitting here, when I heard a voice cry 'Halloa! Below there!' I stared up, looked from that door, and saw this someone else standing by the red light near the tunnel, waving as I just now showed you. The voice seemed hoarse with shouting, and it cried, 'Look out! Look out!' And then again 'Halloa! Below there! Look out!' I caught up my lamp, turned it on red, and ran towards the figure, calling, 'What's wrong? What has happened? Where?' It stood just outside the blackness of the tunnel. I advanced so close upon it that I wondered at its keeping the sleeve across its eyes. I ran right up at it, and had my hand stretched out to pull the sleeve away, when it was gone."

"Into the tunnel," said I.

"No. I ran on into the tunnel, five hundred yards. I stopped and held my lamp above my head, and saw the figures of the measured distance, and saw the wet stains stealing down the walls and trickling through the arch. I ran out again, faster than I had run in (for I had a mortal abhorrence of the place upon me), and I looked all round the red light with my own red light, and I went up the iron ladder to the gallery atop of it, and I came down again, and ran back here.

I telegraphed both ways, 'An alarm has been given. Is anything wrong?' The answer came back, both ways: 'All well.'"

Resisting the slow touch of a frozen finger tracing out my spine, I showed him how that this figure must be a deception of his sense of sight, and how that figures, originating in disease of the delicate nerves that minister to the functions of the eye, were known to have often troubled patients, some of whom had become conscious of the nature of their affliction, and had even proved it by experiments upon themselves. "As to an imaginary cry," said I, "do but listen for a moment to the wind in this unnatural valley while we speak so low, and to the wild harp it makes of the telegraph wires!"

That was all very well, he returned, after we had sat listening for a while, and he ought to know something of the wind and the wires, he who so often passed long winter nights there, alone and watching. But he would beg to remark that he had not finished.

I asked his pardon, and he slowly added these words, touching my arm:

"Within six hours after the appearance, the memorable accident on this Line happened, and within ten hours the dead and wounded were brought along through the tunnel over the spot where the figure had stood."

A disagreeable shudder crept over me, but I did my best against it. It was not to be denied, I rejoined, that this was a remarkable coincidence, calculated deeply to impress his mind. But it was unquestionable that remarkable coincidences did continually occur, and they must be taken into account in dealing with such a subject. Though to be sure I must admit, I added (for I thought I saw that he was going to bring the objection to bear upon me), men of common sense did not allow much for coincidences in making the ordinary calculations of life.

He again begged to remark that he had not finished.

I again begged his pardon for being betrayed into interruptions.

"This," he said, again laying his hand upon my arm, and glancing over his shoulder with hollow eyes, "was just a year ago. Six or seven months passed, and I had recovered from the surprise and shock, when one morning, as the day was breaking, I, standing at that door, looked towards the red light, and saw the spectre again." He stopped, with a fixed look at me.

"Did it cry out?"

"No. It was silent."

"Did it wave its arm?"

"No. It leaned against the shaft of the light, with both hands before the face. Like this."

Once more, I followed his action with my eyes. It was an action of mourning. I have seen such an attitude in stone figures on tombs.

"Did you go up to it?"

"I came in and sat down, partly to collect my thoughts, partly because it had turned me faint. When I went to the door again, daylight was above me, and the ghost was gone."

"But nothing followed? Nothing came of this?"

He touched me on the arm with his forefinger twice or thrice, giving a ghastly nod each time:

"That very day, as a train came out of the tunnel, I noticed, at a carriage window on my side, what looked like a confusion of hands and heads, and something waved. I saw it, just in time to signal the driver, Stop! He shut off, and put his brake on, but the train drifted past here a hundred and fifty yards or more. I ran after it, and, as I went along, heard terrible screams and cries. A beautiful young lady had died instantaneously in one of the compartments, and was brought in here, and laid down on this floor between us."

Involuntarily, I pushed my chair back, as I looked from the boards at which he pointed, to himself.

"True, sir. True. Precisely as it happened, so I tell it you."

I could think of nothing to say, to any purpose, and my mouth was very dry. The wind and the wires took up the story with a long lamenting wail.

He resumed. "Now, sir, mark this, and judge how my mind is troubled. The spectre came back, a week ago. Ever since, it has been there, now and again, by fits and starts."

"At the light?"

"At the Danger-light."

"What does it seem to do?"

He repeated, if possible with increased passion and vehemence, that former gesticulation of "For God's sake clear the way!"

Then, he went on. "I have no peace or rest for it. It calls to me for many minutes together, in an agonized manner, 'Below there! Look out! Look out!' It stands waving to me. It rings my little bell——"

I caught at that. "Did it ring your bell yesterday evening when I was here, and you went to the door?"

"Twice."

"Why, see," said I, "how your imagination misleads you. My eyes were on the bell, and my ears were open to the bell, and if I am a living man, it did *not* ring at those times. No, nor at any other time, except when it was rung in the natural course of physical things by the station communicating with you."

He shook his head. "I have never made a mistake as to that, yet, sir. I have never confused the spectre's ring with the man's. The ghost's ring is a strange vibration in the bell that it derives from nothing else, and I have not asserted that the bell stirs to the eye. I don't wonder that you failed to hear it. But *I* heard it."

"And did the spectre seem to be there, when you looked out."

"It was there."

"Both times?"

He repeated firmly: "Both times."

"Will you come to the door with me, and look for it now?"

He bit his underlip as though he were somewhat unwilling, but arose. I opened the door, and stood on the step, while he stood in the doorway. There, was the Danger-light. There, was the dismal mouth of the tunnel. There, were the high wet stone walls of the cutting. There, were the stars above them.

"Do you see it?" I asked him, taking particular note of his face. His eyes were prominent and strained; but not very much more so, perhaps, than my own had been when I had directed them earnestly towards the same spot.

"No," he answered. "It is not there."

"Agreed," said I.

We went in again, shut the door, and resumed our seats. I was thinking how best to improve this advantage, if it might be called one, when he took up the conversation in such a matter of course way, so assuming that there could be no serious question of fact between us, that I felt myself placed in the weakest of positions.

"By this time you will fully understand, sir," he said, "that what troubles me so dreadfully, is the question, What does the spectre mean?"

I was not sure, I told him, that I did fully understand.

"What is its warning against?" he said, ruminating, with his eyes on the fire, and only by times turning them on me. "What is the danger? Where is the danger? There is danger overhanging, somewhere on the Line. Some dreadful calamity will happen. It is not to be doubted this third time, after what has gone before. But surely this is a cruel haunting of *me*. What can *I* do?"

He pulled out his handkerchief, and wiped the drops from his heated forehead.

"If I telegraph Danger, on either side of me, or on both, I can give no reason for it," he went on, wiping the palms of his hands. "I should get into trouble, and do no good. They would think I was mad. This is the way it would work: Message: 'Danger! Take care!' Answer: 'What danger? Where?' Message: 'Don't know. But for God's sake take care!' They would displace me. What else could they do?"

His pain of mind was most pitiable to see. It was the mental torture of a conscientious man, oppressed beyond endurance by an unintelligible responsibility involving life.

"When it first stood under the Danger-light," he went on, putting his dark hair back from his head, and drawing his hands outwards across and across his temples in an extremity of feverish distress, "why not tell me where that accident was to happen—if it must happen? Why not tell me how it could be averted—if it could have been averted? When on its second coming it hid its face, why not tell me instead: 'She is going to die. Let them keep her at home'? If it came, on those two occasions, only to show me that its warnings were true, and so to prepare me for the third, why not warn me plainly now? And I, Lord help me! A mere poor signal-man on this solitary station! Why not go to somebody with credit to be believed, and power to act!"

When I saw him in this state, I saw that for the poor man's sake, as well as for the public safety, what I had to do for the time was, to compose his mind. Therefore, setting aside all question of reality or unreality between us, I represented to him that whoever thoroughly discharged his duty, must do well, and that at least it was his comfort that he understood his duty, though he did not understand these confounding appearances. In this effort I succeeded far better than in the attempt to reason him out of his conviction. He became calm; the occupations incidental to his post as the night advanced, began to make larger demands on his attention; and I left him at two in the morning. I had offered to stay through the night, but he would not hear of it.

That I more than once looked back at the red light as I ascended the pathway, that I did not like the red light, and that I should have slept but poorly if my bed had been under it, I see no reason to conceal. Nor did I like the two sequences of the accident and the dead girl. I see no reason to conceal that, either.

But, what ran most in my thoughts was the consideration how ought I to act, having become the recipient of this disclosure? I had proved the man to be intelligent, vigilant, painstaking and exact; but how long might he remain so, in his state of mind? Though in a subordinate position, still he held a most important trust, and would I (for instance) like to stake my own life on the chances of his continuing to execute it with precision?

Unable to overcome a feeling that there would be something treacherous in my communicating what he had told me to his superiors in the company, without first being plain with himself and proposing a middle course to him, I ultimately resolved to offer to accompany him (otherwise keeping his secret for the present) to the wisest medical practitioner we could hear of in those parts, and to take his opinion. A change in his time of duty would come round next night, he had apprised me, and he would be off an hour or two after sunrise, and on again soon after sunset. I had appointed to return accordingly.

Next evening was a lovely evening, and I walked out early to enjoy it. The sun was not yet quite down when I traversed the field-path near the top of the deep cutting. I would extend my walk for an hour, I said to myself, half an hour on and half an hour back, and it would then be time to go to my signal-man's box.

Before pursuing my stroll, I stepped to the brink, and mechanically looked down, from the point from which I had first seen him. I cannot describe the thrill that seized upon me, when, close at the mouth of the tunnel, I saw the appearance of a man, with his left sleeve across his eyes, passionately waving his right arm.

The nameless horror that oppressed me, passed in a moment, for in a moment I saw that this appearance of a man was a man indeed, and that there was a little group of other men standing at a short distance, to whom he seemed to be rehearsing the gesture he made. The Danger-light was not yet lighted. Against its shaft, a little low hut, entirely new to me, had been made of some wooden supports and tarpaulin. It looked no bigger than a bed.

With an irresistible sense that something was wrong—with a flashing self-reproachful fear that fatal mischief had come of my leaving the man there, and causing no one to be sent to overlook or correct what he did—I descended the notched path with all the speed I could make.

"What is the matter?" I asked the men.

"Signal-man killed this morning, sir."

"Not the man belonging to that box?"

"Yes, sir."

"Not the man I know?"

"You will recognize him, sir, if you knew him," said the man who spoke for the others, solemnly uncovering his own head and raising an end of the tarpaulin, "for his face is quite composed."

"O! how did this happen, how did this happen?" I asked, turning from one to another as the hut closed in again.

"He was cut down by an engine, sir. No man in England knew his work better. But somehow he was not clear of the outer rail. It was just at broad day. He had struck the light, and had the lamp in his hand. As the engine came out of the tunnel, his back was towards her, and she cut him down. That man drove her, and was showing how it happened. Show the gentleman, Tom."

The man who wore a rough dark dress, stepped back to his former place at the mouth of the tunnel!

"Coming round the curve in the tunnel, sir," he said, "I saw him at the end, like as if I saw him down a perspective-glass. There was no time to check speed, and I knew him to be very careful. As he didn't seem to take heed of the whistle, I shut it off when we were running down upon him, and called to him as loud as I could call."

"What did you say?"

"I said, Below there! Look out! Look out! For God's sake clear the way!"

I started.

"Ah! it was a dreadful time, sir. I never left off calling to him. I put this arm before my eyes, not to see, and I waved this arm to the last; but it was no use."

* * *

Without prolonging the narrative to dwell on any one of its curious circumstances more than on any other, I may, in closing it, point out the coincidence that the warning of the engine-driver included, not only the words which the unfortunate signal-man had repeated to me as haunting him, but also the words which I myself—not he—had attached, and that only in my own mind, to the gesticulation he had imitated.

# The Facts in the Case of M. Valdemar

*Edgar Allan Poe*

Of course I shall not pretend to consider it any matter for wonder, that the extraordinary case of M. Valdemar has excited discussion. It would have been a miracle had it not—especially under the circumstances. Through the desire of all parties concerned, to keep the affair from the public, at least for the present, or until we had further opportunities for investigation—through our endeavors to effect this—a garbled or exaggerated account made its way into society, and became the source of many unpleasant misrepresentations; and, very naturally, of a great deal of disbelief.

It is now rendered necessary that I give the *facts*—as far as I comprehend them myself. They are, succinctly, these:

My attention, for the last three years, had been repeatedly drawn to the subject of Mesmerism; and, about nine months ago, it occurred to me, quite suddenly, that in the series of experiments made hitherto, there had been a very remarkable and most unaccountable omission:—no person had as yet been mesmerized *in articulo mortis.* It remained to be seen, first, whether, in such condition, there existed in the patient any susceptibility to the magnetic influence; secondly, whether, if any existed, it was impaired or increased by the condition; thirdly, to what extent, or for how long a period, the encroachments of Death might be arrested by the process. There were other points to be ascertained, but these most excited my curiosity—the last in especial, from the immensely important character of its consequences.

In looking around me for some subject by whose means I might test these particulars, I was brought to think of my friend, M. Ernest Valdemar, the well-known compiler of the "Bibliotheca Forensica," and author (under the *nom de plume* of Issachar Marx) of the Polish versions of "Wallenstein" and "Gargantua." M. Valdemar, who has resided principally at Harlem, N. Y., since the year of 1839, is (or was) particularly noticeable for the extreme spareness of his person—

his lower limbs much resembling those of John Randolph; and, also, for the whiteness of his whiskers, in violent contrast to the blackness of his hair—the latter, in consequence, being very generally mistaken for a wig. His temperament was markedly nervous, and rendered him a good subject for mesmeric experiment. On two or three occasions I had put him to sleep with little difficulty, but was disappointed in other results which his peculiar constitution had naturally led me to anticipate. His will was at no period positively, or thoroughly, under my control, and in regard to *clairvoyance*, I could accomplish with him nothing to be relied upon. I always attributed my failure at these points to the disordered state of his health. For some months previous to my becoming acquainted with him, his physicians had declared him in a confirmed phthisis. It was his custom, indeed, to speak calmly of his approaching dissolution, as of a matter neither to be avoided nor regretted.

When the ideas to which I have alluded first occurred to me, it was of course very natural that I should think of M. Valdemar. I knew the steady philosophy of the man too well to apprehend any scruples from *him*; and he had no relatives in America who would be likely to interfere. I spoke to him frankly upon the subject; and, to my surprise, his interest seemed vividly excited. I say to my surprise; for, although he had always yielded his person freely to my experiments, he had never

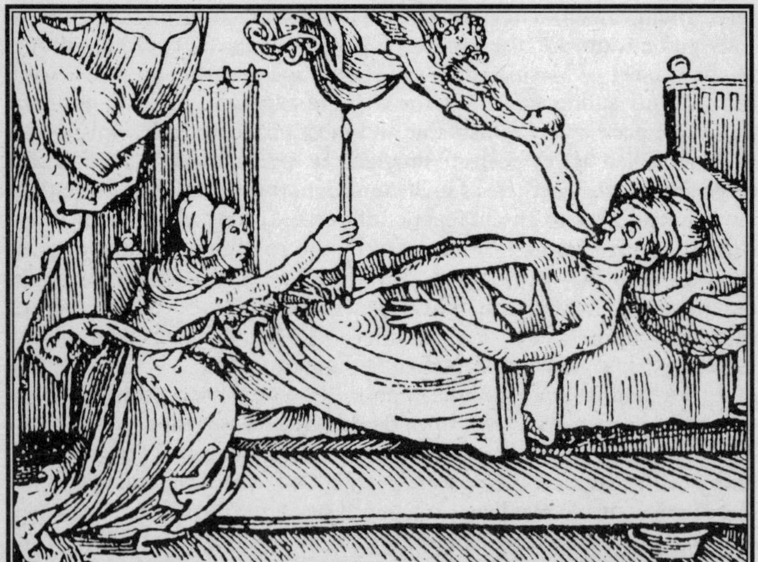

before given me any tokens of sympathy with what I did. His disease was of that character which would admit of exact calculation in respect to the epoch of its termination in death; and it was finally arranged between us that he would send for me about twenty-four hours before the period announced by his physicians as that of his decease.

It is now rather more than seven months since I received, from M. Valdemar himself, the subjoined note:

"*My Dear P*——

"*You may as well come now. D*—— *and F*—— *are agreed that I cannot hold out beyond to-morrow midnight; and I think they have hit the time very nearly.*

*Valdemar*"

I received this note within half an hour after it was written, and in fifteen minutes more I was in the dying man's chamber. I had not seen him for ten days, and was appalled by the fearful alteration which the brief interval had wrought in him. His face wore a leaden hue; the eyes were utterly lustreless; and the emaciation was so extreme, that the skin had been broken through by the cheekbones. His expectoration was excessive. The pulse was barely perceptible. He retained, nevertheless, in a very remarkable manner, both his mental power and a certain degree of physical strength. He spoke with distinctness—took some palliative medicines without aid—and, when I entered the room, was occupied in penciling memoranda in a pocket-book. He was propped up in the bed by pillows. Doctors D—— and F—— were in attendance.

After pressing Valdemar's hand, I took these gentlemen aside, and obtained from them a minute account of the patient's condition. The left lung had been for eighteen months in a semi-osseous or cartilaginous state, and was, of course, entirely useless for all purposes of vitality. The right, in its upper portion, was also partially, if not thoroughly, ossified, while the lower region was merely a mass of purulent tubercles, running one into another. Several extensive perforations existed; and, at one point, permanent adhesion to the ribs had taken place. These appearances in the right lobe were of comparatively recent date. The ossification had proceeded with very unusual rapidity; no sign of it had been discovered a month before, and the adhesion had only been observed during the three previous days. Independently of the phthisis, the patient was suspected of aneurism of the aorta; but on this point the osseous symptoms rendered an exact diagnosis impossible. It was the opinion of both physicians that M. Valdemar would die about midnight on the morrow (Sunday). It was then seven o'clock on Saturday evening.

On quitting the invalid's bedside to hold conversation with myself, Doctors D— and F— had bidden him a final farewell. It had not been their intention to return; but, at my request, they agreed to look in upon the patient about ten the next night.

When they had gone, I spoke freely with M. Valdemar on the subject of his approaching dissolution, as well as, more particularly, of the experiment proposed. He still professed himself quite willing and even anxious to have it made, and urged me to commence it at once. A male and a female nurse were in attendance; but I did not feel myself altogether at liberty to engage in a task of this character with no more reliable witnesses than these people, in case of sudden accident, might prove. I therefore postponed operations until about eight the next night, when the arrival of a medical student, with whom I had some acquaintance (Mr. Theodore L—l), relieved me from further embarrassment. It had been my design, originally, to wait for the physicians; but I was induced to proceed, first, by the urgent entreaties of M. Valdemar, and secondly, by my conviction that I had not a moment to lose, as he was evidently sinking fast.

Mr. L—l was so kind as to accede to my desire that he would take notes of all that occurred; and it is from his memoranda that what I now have to relate is, for the most part, either condensed or copied *verbatim.*

It wanted about five minutes of eight when, taking the patient's hand, I begged him to state, as distinctly as he could, to Mr. L—l, whether he (M. Valdemar) was entirely willing that I should make the experiment of mesmerizing him in his then condition.

He replied feebly, yet quite audibly: "Yes, I wish to be mesmerized"—adding immediately afterward: "I fear you have deferred it too long."

While he spoke thus, I commenced the passes which I had already found most effectual in subduing him. He was evidently influenced with the first lateral stroke of my hand across his forehead; but, although I exerted all my powers, no further perceptible effect was induced until some minutes after ten o'clock, when Doctors D— and F— called, according to appointment. I explained to them, in a few words, what I designed, and as they opposed no objection, saying that the patient was already in the death agony, I proceeded without hesitation—exchanging, however, the lateral passes for downward ones, and directing my gaze entirely into the right eye of the sufferer.

By this time his pulse was imperceptible and his breathing was stertorous, and at intervals of half a minute.

This condition was nearly unaltered for a quarter of an hour. At the expiration of this period, however, a natural although a very deep sigh escaped from the bosom of the dying man, and the stertorous breathing ceased—that is to say, its stertorousness was no longer apparent; the intervals were undiminished. The patient's extremities were of an icy coldness.

At five minutes before eleven, I perceived unequivocal signs of the mesmeric influence. The glassy roll of the eye was changed for that expression of uneasy *inward* examination which is never seen except in cases of sleep-waking, and which it is quite impossible to mistake. With a few rapid lateral passes I made the lids quiver, as in incipient sleep, and with a few more I closed them altogether. I was not satisfied, however, with this, but continued the manipulations vigorously, and with the fullest exertion of the will, until I had completely stiffened the limbs of the slumberer, after placing them in a seemingly easy position. The legs were at full length; the arms were nearly so, and reposed on the bed at a moderate distance from the loins. The head was very slightly elevated.

When I had accomplished this, it was fully midnight, and I requested the gentlemen present to examine M. Valdemar's condition. After a few experiments, they admitted him to be in an unusually perfect state of mesmeric trance. The curiosity of both the physicians was greatly excited. Dr. D—— resolved at once to remain with the patient all night, while Dr. F—— took leave with a promise to return at daybreak. Mr. L——l and the nurses remained.

We left M. Valdemar entirely undisturbed until about three o'clock in the morning, when I approached him and found him in precisely the same condition as when Dr. F—— went away—that is to say, he lay in the same position; the pulse was imperceptible; the breathing was gentle (scarcely noticeable, unless through the application of a mirror to the lips); the eyes were closed naturally; and the limbs were as rigid and as cold as marble. Still, the general appearance was certainly not that of death.

As I approached M. Valdemar I made a kind of half effort to influence his right arm into pursuit of my own, as I passed the latter gently to and fro above his person. In such experiments with this patient, I had never perfectly succeeded before, and assuredly I had little thought of succeeding now; but to my astonishment, his arm very readily, although feebly, followed every direction I assigned it with mine. I determined to hazard a few words of conversation.

"M. Valdemar," I said, "are you asleep?" He made no answer, but I perceived a tremor about the lips, and was thus induced to repeat the question, again and again. At its third repetition, his whole frame was agitated by a very slight shivering; the eyelids unclosed themselves so far as to display a white line of a ball; the lips moved sluggishly, and from between them, in a barely audible whisper, issued the words:

"Yes;—asleep now. Do not wake me!—let me die so!"

I here felt the limbs, and found them as rigid as ever. The right arm, as before, obeyed the direction of my hand. I questioned the sleep-waker again:

"Do you still feel pain in the breast, M. Valdemar?"

The answer now was immediate, but even less audible than before:

"No pain—I am dying!"

I did not think it advisable to disturb him further just then, and nothing more was said or done until the arrival of Dr. F—, who came a little before sunrise, and expressed unbounded astonishment at finding the patient still alive. After feeling the pulse and applying a mirror to the lips, he requested me to speak to the sleep-waker again. I did so, saying:

"M. Valdemar, do you still sleep?"

As before, some minutes elapsed ere a reply was made; and during the interval the dying man seemed to be collecting his energies to speak. At my fourth repetition of the question, he said very faintly, almost inaudibly:

"Yes; still asleep—dying."

It was now the opinion, or rather the wish, of the physicians, that M. Valdemar should be suffered to remain undisturbed in his present apparently tranquil condition, until death should supervene—and this, it was generally agreed, must now take place within a few minutes. I concluded, however, to speak to him once more, and merely repeated my previous question.

While I spoke, there came a marked change over the countenance of the sleep-waker. The eyes rolled themselves slowly open, the pupils disappearing upwardly; the skin generally assumed a cadaverous hue, resembling not so much parchment as white paper; and the circular hectic spots which, hitherto, had been strongly defined in the centre of each cheek, *went out* at once. I use this expression, because the suddenness of their departure put me in mind of nothing so much as the extinguishment of a candle by a puff of the breath. The upper lip, at the same time, writhed itself away from the teeth, which it had previously covered completely; while the lower jaw fell with an audible jerk, leaving the mouth widely extended, and disclosing in full view the swollen and blackened tongue. I presume that no member of the party then present had been unaccustomed to death-bed horrors, but so hideous beyond conception was the appearance of M. Valdemar at this moment, that there was a general shrinking back from the region of the bed.

I now feel that I have reached a point of this narrative at which every reader will be startled into positive disbelief. It is my business, however, simply to proceed.

There was no longer the faintest sign of vitality in M. Valdemar; and concluding him to be dead, we were consigning him to the charge of the nurses, when a strong vibratory motion was observable in the tongue. This continued for perhaps a minute. At the expiration of this period, there issued from the distended and motionless jaws a voice—such as it would be madness in me to attempt describing. There are, indeed, two or three epithets which might be considered as applicable to it in part; I might say, for example, that the sound was harsh, and broken and hollow; but the hideous whole is indescribable, for the simple reason that no similar sounds have ever jarred upon the ear of humanity. There were two particulars, nevertheless, which I thought then, and still think, might fairly be stated as characteristic of the intonation—as well adapted to convey some idea of its unearthly peculiarity. In the first place, the voice seemed to reach our ears—at least mine—from a vast distance, or from some deep cavern within the earth. In the second place, it impressed me (I fear, indeed, that it will be impossible to make myself comprehended) as gelatinous or glutinous matters impress the sense of touch.

I have spoken both of "sound" and of "voice." I mean to say that the sound was one of distinct—of even wonderfully, thrillingly distinct—syllabification. M. Valdemar *spoke*—obviously in reply to the question I had propounded to him a few minutes before. I had asked him, it will be remembered, if he still slept. He now said:

"Yes;—no;—I *have been* sleeping—and now—now—*I am dead.*"

No person present even affected to deny, or attempted to repress, the unutterable, shuddering horror which these few words, thus uttered, were so well calculated to convey. Mr. L——l (the student) swooned. The nurses immediately left the chamber, and could not be induced to return. My own impressions I would not pretend to render intelligible to the reader. For nearly an hour, we busied ourselves, silently—without the utterance of a word—in endeavors to revive Mr. L——l. When he came to himself, we addressed ourselves again to an investigation of M. Valdemar's condition.

It remained in all respects as I have last described it, with the exception that the mirror no longer afforded evidence of respiration. An attempt to draw blood from the arm failed. I should mention, too, that this limb was no further subject to my will. I endeavored in vain to make it follow the direction of my hand. The only real indication, indeed, of the mesmeric influence, was not found in the vibratory movement of the tongue, whenever I addressed M. Valdemar a question. He seemed to be making an effort to reply, but had no longer sufficient volition. To queries put to him by any other person than myself he seemed utterly insensible—although I endeavored to place each member of the company in mesmeric *rapport* with him. I believe that I have now related all that is necessary to an understanding of the sleep-waker's state at this epoch. Other nurses were procured; and at ten o'clock I left the house in company with the two physicians and Mr. L——l.

In the afternoon we all called again to see the patient. His condition remained precisely the same. We had now some discussion as to the propriety and feasibility of awakening him; but we had little difficulty in agreeing that no good purpose would be served by so doing. It was evident that, so far, death (or what is usually termed death) had been arrested by the mesmeric process. It seemed clear to us all that to awaken M. Valdemar would be merely to insure his instant, or at least his speedy, dissolution.

From this period until the close of last week—*an interval of nearly seven months*—we continued to make daily calls at M. Valdemar's house, accompanied, now and then, by medical and other friends. All this time the sleep-waker remained *exactly* as I have last described him. The nurses' attentions were continual.

It was on Friday last that we finally resolved to make the experiment of awakening, or attempting to awaken him; and it is the (perhaps) unfortunate result of this latter experiment which has given rise to so much discussion in private circles—to so much of what I cannot help thinking unwarranted popular feeling.

For the purpose of relieving M. Valdemar from the mesmeric trance, I made use of the customary passes. These for a time were unsuccessful. The first indication of revival was afforded by a partial descent of the iris. It was observed, as especially remarkable, that this lowering of the pupil was accompanied by the profuse out-flowing of a yellowish ichor (from beneath the lids) of a pungent and highly offensive odor.

It was now suggested that I should attempt to influence the patient's arm as heretofore. I made the attempt and failed. Dr. F—— then intimated a desire to have me put a question. I did so, as follows:

"M. Valdemar, can you explain to us what are your feelings or wishes now?"

There was an instant return of the hectic circles on the cheeks: the tongue quivered, or rather rolled violently in the mouth (although the jaws and lips remained rigid as before), and at length the same hideous voice which I have already described, broke forth:

"For God's sake!—quick!—quick!—put me to sleep—or, quick!—waken me!—quick!—*I say to you that I am dead!*"

I was thoroughly unnerved, and for an instant remained undecided what to do. At first I made an endeavor to recompose the patient; but; failing in this through total abeyance of the will, I retraced my steps and as earnestly struggled to awaken him. In this attempt I soon saw that I should be successful—or at least I soon fancied that my success would be complete—and I am sure that all in the room were prepared to see the patient awaken.

For what really occurred, however, it is quite impossible that any human being could have been prepared.

As I rapidly made the mesmeric passes, amid ejaculations of "dead! dead!" absolutely *bursting* from the tongue and not from the lips of the sufferer, his whole frame at once—within the space of a single minute, or less, shrunk—crumbled—absolutely *rotted* away beneath my hands. Upon the bed, before that whole company, there lay a nearly liquid mass of loathsome—of detestable putrescence.

# The Hand

*Guy de Maupassant*

We were all seated round Monsieur Bermutier, the magistrate, who was giving us his opinion on the affair at St Cloud. The inexplicable crime had convulsed Paris for a whole month, yet no single being had solved the mystery.

Upright, with his back to the fireplace, Monsieur Bermutier held forth, marshalled proofs, and discussed divers opinions, but he came to no conclusion.

Several of the women present had risen from their seats to be nearer to him; and they remained standing, their eyes fixed on the clean-shaven lips whence issued such words of grave import. They thrilled and shuddered, devoured with curiosity and with that avid and insatiable love of the horrible that haunts their souls and tortures them like hunger.

One, paler than the others, broke the silence:

"It is terrible! It is almost supernatural! We shall never know anything about it."

The magistrate turned to her:

"You are right, madame; it is quite probable we shall never know anything about it. But the word 'supernatural' that you used a moment ago has no meaning in this case. We have before us a crime very ably conceived and very ably carried out, so wrapped in mystery that we are unable to dissociate it from the impenetrable circumstances surrounding it. But in times gone by I had to follow up a case where the fantastic element was really intermingled. We had to abandon it, however, as no one was able to throw any light on it."

Breathlessly, and as if with one voice, several of the ladies exclaimed:

"Oh, do tell us about it!"

Monsieur Bermutier smiled gravely, as befits a magistrate, and continued:

You must not think for a moment that I fancied there was any element of the supernatural in this case. I am no believer in the abnormal. But if, instead of using the word "supernatural" to explain what we do not understand, we were to use the word "inexplicable", it would be far better. At any rate, in the tale I am about to relate to you it was mainly the surrounding circumstances, the preparatory circumstances, so to speak, which affected me. Briefly, these are the facts:

In those days I was resident magistrate at Ajaccio, a little white town nestled on the borders of a beautiful gulf, and surrounded by high mountains.

What I had principally to deal with were cases of vendetta. There were some that were really magnificent, others excessively dramatic, savage, and again heroic. The most splendid subjects of revenge that a man may dream of—time-honoured hatreds momentarily appeased, perhaps, but never really extinguished—abominably cunning tricks, murder swelling into massacre, and actions almost noble.

For two years I heard of nothing but the price of blood, of the terrible Corsican law which enforces vengeance on the evil-doer to be borne by his descendants and near relations. I had seen old men, children, and cousins with their throats cut. My brain teemed with such happenings.

One day I heard that an Englishman had rented a little villa on the edge of the gulf for several years. He had brought a French manservant with him, picked up on the way at Marseilles. Soon everyone was talking of this queer foreigner, who lived alone in his house; leaving it only to hunt and fish. He never spoke to anyone, never entered the town, and practised shooting every morning for two or three hours with pistol and rifle.

Stories were rife about him. Some made out he was a great personage who had fled his country for political reasons, others affirmed that he was in hiding for having committed a terrible crime. They even cited the particularly horrible details.

In my position as magistrate I wanted to gain some information about this man, but I failed to learn anything at all. He gave his name as Sir John Rowell.

So I had to be content to watch him closely, but, to speak candidly, my attention was called to nothing suspicious about him. However, as the rumours about him continued, swelled, and became common talk, I resolved to see him for myself; and I set about shooting regularly in his neighbourhood.

For a long while I awaited an opportunity. At last it came, in the shape of a partridge which I shot and killed under the Englishman's nose. My dog brought it to me. Taking the bird, I went and excused myself for my want of manners, and begged Sir John Rowell to accept the dead bird.

He was a huge man, red-haired and red-bearded, very tall, very big, a placid and polite Hercules. He had none of that so-called British stiffness; and he thanked me warmly for my small civility in French with an accent from over the water. After a month had gone by we had spoken five or six times together.

At length one evening as I passed his door and I saw him sitting in his garden, astride a chair, smoking a pipe, I bowed, and he invited me to come in and drink a glass of beer. I did not wait to be asked twice.

He received me with the meticulous courtesy of an Englishman, spoke warmly of France and Corsica, declaring that he liked both country and seashore extremely.

Then cautiously I put to him some leading questions under the guise of a lively interest in his life and doings. He answered without any embarrassment, told me that he had travelled much in Africa, India, and America, and added, laughing:

"Oh, I had many adventures!"

Then I talked sport, and he gave me some exceedingly curious details gathered in the pursuit of the hippopotamus, the tiger, the elephant, and even the gorilla.

"Those are all formidable beasts?" said I.

He smiled and replied:

"Oh, no; man was the worst!"

And he laughed outright, with the hearty laugh of a satisfied Englishman.

"Man was often my game," he added.

Then he spoke of arms, and invited me to come in and look at some rifles of different makes. His sitting-room was hung with black—black silk embroidered with gold. Large yellow flowers sprawled over the dark stuff, and shone like fire. The stuff was Japanese, he told me.

In the centre of the largest panel something extraordinary caught my eye. A black object stood out in relief against a square of red velvet. I went up to it. It was a hand—a man's hand! No bleached and well-cleaned skeleton hand, but a dried-up black hand, with its yellow nails, its bared muscles, and traces of dried blood—blood smeared like mud on the bones—cut off cleanly as if by a hatchet in the middle of the forearm.

Round the wrist a heavy iron chain was riveted, welded to this unclean member, and holding it fast to the wall with a ring strong enough to hold an elephant in leash.

"What is that?" I asked.

"He was my deadliest foe," replied the Englishman quietly. "It came from America. It was cut off with a sword, the skin torn away with a flint, and then dried in the sun for a week. A good stroke of work on my part."

I touched this remnant of humanity; it must have belonged to a colossus. The exaggeratedly long fingers were attached by tremendous tendons, which bore scraps of skin here and there. The hand was horrible to look at, skinned thus; it made one's thoughts turn instinctively to some savage and ferocious form of revenge.

"He must have been a very strong man," said I.

"Yes," answered the Englishman calmly; "but I proved the stronger. I put on that chain to hold him fast."

Thinking he was speaking in fun, I said:

"But that chain is of no use now: the hand will not try and escape."

"It has always wanted to go; that chain was necessary," gravely replied Sir John Rowell.

I looked at him with a rapid glance. Had I to deal with a madman, or did he but joke in very bad taste?

His face remained impenetrable, tranquil, and good-natured. I spoke of other things. I admired his guns. I observed, however, that three loaded revolvers lay about the room, as if this man lived in constant dread of being attacked.

I went to see him several times again; then I went no more. We had become used to his presence; he had become a matter of indifference to all.

A whole year slipped by. Then one morning towards the end of November my servant woke me, telling me that Sir John Rowell had been murdered during the night.

Half an hour later I entered the Englishman's house, accompanied by the Commissioner and the Chief Inspector of Police. Overcome with grief, and half distracted, the manservant stood crying in the doorway. At first I suspected the man, but he was innocent. We were never able to find the murderer.

The first thing I saw on entering Sir John's sitting-room was the body lying on its back in the middle of the room. The waistcoat was torn; one sleeve hung in ribbons; there was every sign that a terrible struggle had taken place.

The Englishman had died of strangulation. His black and swollen face, terrifying, seemed to wear an expression of awful fear. He held something between his clenched teeth; and the throat, pierced with five holes that might have been made with fangs of iron, was covered with blood.

A doctor had joined us. Lengthily he examined the marks of fingers on the flesh, and then queerly remarked:

"One might think he had been strangled by a skeleton."

A shudder ran down my spine, and I looked towards the wall at the spot where I had seen the horrible skinned hand. It was no longer there. The chain hung down, broken.

Then I stooped over the dead man, and found between the tense jaws a finger from the hand that had disappeared, cut, or rather sawn, by the teeth just at the second joint.

Inquiries were instituted. Nothing was discovered. Neither door, window, nor furniture had been tampered with. The two watchdogs had not been aroused.

Here, briefly, is the manservant's testimony. For a month past his master had appeared restless. He had received many letters, burnt as soon as received.

In a rage which approached madness he would often take up his whip and furiously beat the shrivelled hand chained to the wall, and which had been removed, no one knew now, at the hour of the crime.

He went to bed very late, and locked himself in with care. He always had firearms within reach of his hand. Often in the night he was heard speaking with raised voice, as if he were quarrelling with someone.

That night, by chance, he had made no sound; and it was only on coming to open the windows that the servant had discovered Sir John lying murdered. He suspected no one.

I told the officers of the law all I knew of the dead man, and a minute inquiry was instituted all over the island. They discovered nothing.

Now, it happened one night three months after the crime had taken place I had a most horrible nightmare. I thought I saw the hand, the sinister hand, run like a scorpion or a spider along my curtains and walls. Three times did I wake, three times did I fall asleep; three times did I see the hideous thing gallop round my room, moving its fingers like feet.

The following day they brought it to me, found in the cemetery on the grave of Sir John Rowell, who had been laid there as we failed to discover his family. The first finger was missing. That, ladies, is my story. I know no more.

The women were all shuddering, terror-struck, and pale.

"But," exclaimed one, "that cannot be the end; that is no explanation! We shall none of us close our eyes tonight if you do not tell us what you think occurred."

The magistrate smiled as he answered reprovingly:

"For my part, madame, I shall certainly spoil your horror-filled dreams, for I merely think that the rightful owner of the hand was not dead, and that he came to seek it with the one left to him. But I was unable to find out how he went about it. That was a kind of vendetta."

One of the women murmured:

"No; it could not have been that!"

"I told you my explanation would not satisfy you", said the magistrate, still smiling.

# The Body Snatcher

*Robert Louis Stevenson*

Every night in the year, four of us sat in the small parlour of the George at Debenham—the undertaker, and the landlord, and Fettes, and myself. Sometimes there would be more; but blow high, blow low, come rain or snow or frost, we four would be each planted in his own particular armchair. Fettes was an old drunken Scotsman, a man of education obviously, and a man of some property, since he lived in idleness. He had come to Debenham years ago, while still young, and by a mere continuance of living had grown to be an adopted townsman. His blue camlet cloak was a local antiquity, like the church-spire. His place in the parlour at the George, his absence from the church, his old, crapulous, disreputable vices, were all things of course in Debenham. He had some vague Radical opinions and some fleeting infidelities, which he would now and again set forth and emphasize with tottering slaps upon the table. He drank rum—five glasses regularly every evening; and for the greater portion of his nightly visit to the George sat, with his glass in his right hand, in a state of melancholy alcoholic saturation. We called him the Doctor, for he was supposed to have some special knowledge of medicine and had been known, upon a pinch, to set a fracture or reduce a dislocation; but beyond these slight particulars, we had no knowledge of his character and antecedents.

One dark winter night—it had struck nine some time before the landlord joined us—there was a sick man in the George, a great neighbouring proprietor suddenly struck down with apoplexy on his way to Parliament; and the great man's still greater London doctor had been telegraphed to his bedside. It was the first time that such a thing had happened in Debenham, for the railway was but newly open, and we were all proportionately moved by the occurrence.

"He's come," said the landlord, after he had filled and lighted his pipe.

"He?" said I. "Who?—not the doctor?"

"Himself," replied our host.

"What is his name?"

"Dr Macfarlane," said the landlord.

Fettes was far through his third tumbler, stupidly fuddled, now nodding over, now staring mazily around him; but at the last word he seemed to awaken and repeated the name "Macfarlane" twice, quietly enough the first time, but with sudden emotion at the second.

"Yes," said the landlord, "that's his name, Doctor Wolfe Macfarlane."

Fettes became instantly sober; his eyes awoke, his voice became clear, loud and steady, his language forcible and earnest. We were all startled by the transformation, as if a man had risen from the dead.

"I beg your pardon," he said, "I am afraid I have not been paying much attention to your talk. Who is this Wolfe Macfarlane?" And then, when he had heard the landlord out, "It cannot be, it cannot be," he added; "and yet I would like well to see him face to face."

"Do you know him, Doctor?" asked the undertaker, with a gasp.

"God forbid!" was the reply. "And yet the name is a strange one; it were too much to fancy two. Tell me, landlord, is he old?"

"Well," said the host, "he's not a young man, to be sure, and his hair is white, but he looks younger than you."

"He is older, though; years older. But," with a slap upon the table, "it's the rum you see in my face—rum and sin. This man, perhaps, may have an easy conscience and a good digestion. Conscience! Hear me speak. You would think I was some good, old, decent Christian, would you not? But no, not I; I never canted. Voltaire might have canted if he'd stood in my shoes; but the brains"—with a rattling fillip on his bald head—"the brains were clear and active and I saw and made no deductions."

"If you know this doctor," I ventured to remark, after a somewhat awful pause, "I should gather that you do not share the landlord's good opinion."

Fettes paid no regard to me.

"Yes," he said, with sudden decision, "I must see him face to face."

There was another pause and then a door was closed rather sharply on the first floor and a step was heard upon the stair.

"That's the doctor," cried the landlord. "Look sharp and you can catch him."

It was but two steps from the small parlour to the door of the old George inn; the wide oak staircase landed almost in the street; there was room for a Turkey rug and nothing more between the threshold and the last round of the descent; but this little space was every evening brilliantly lit up, not only by the light upon the stair and the great signal-lamp below the sign, but by the warm radiance of the bar-room window. The George thus brightly advertised itself to passers-by in the cold street. Fettes walked steadily to the spot and we, who were hanging behind, beheld the two men meet, as one of them had phrased it, face to face. Dr Macfarlane was alert and vigorous. His white hair set off his pale and placid, although energetic, countenance. He was richly dressed in the finest of broadcloth and the whitest of linen, with a great gold watch-chain, and studs and spectacles of the same precious material. He wore a broad-folded tie, white and speckled with lilac, and he carried on his arm a comfortable driving-coat of fur. There was no doubt but he became his years, breathing, as he did, of wealth and consideration; and it was a surprising contrast to see our parlour sot—bald, dirty, pimpled and robed in his old camlet cloak—confront him at the bottom of the stairs.

"Macfarlane!" he said somewhat loudly, more like a herald than a friend.

The great doctor pulled up short on the fourth step, as though the familiarity of the address surprised and somewhat shocked his dignity.

"Toddy Macfarlane!" repeated Fettes.

The London man almost staggered. He stared for the swiftest of seconds at the man before him, glanced behind him with a sort of scare, and then in a startled whisper, "Fettes!" he said, "you!"

"Ay," said the other, "me! Did you think I was dead too? We are not so easy shut of our acquaintance."

"Hush, hush!" exclaimed the doctor. "Hush, hush! this meeting is so unexpected—I can see you are unmanned. I hardly knew you, I confess, at first, but I am overjoyed—overjoyed to have this opportunity. For the present it must be how-d'ye-do and goodbye in one, for my fly is waiting and I must not fail the train; but you shall—let me see—yes—you shall give me your address and you can count on early news of me. We must do something for you, Fettes. I fear you are out at elbows; but we must see to that for auld lang syne, as once we sang at suppers."

"Money!" cried Fettes; "money from you! The money that I had from you is lying where I cast it in the rain."

Dr Macfarlane had talked himself into some measure of superiority and confidence, but the uncommon energy of this refusal cast him back into his first confusion.

A horrible, ugly look came and went across his almost venerable countenance. "My dear fellow," he said, "be it as you please; my last thought is to offend you. I would intrude on none. I will leave you my address, however——"

"I do not wish it—I do not wish to know the roof that shelters you," interrupted the other. "I heard your name; I feared it might be you; I wished to know if, after all, there were a God; I know now that there is none. Begone!"

He still stood in the middle of the rug, between the stair and the doorway; and the great London physician, in order to escape, would be forced to step to one side. It was plain that he hesitated before the thought of his humiliation. White as he was, there was a dangerous glitter in his spectacles; but while he still paused uncertain, he became aware that the driver of his fly was peering in from the street at this unusual scene and caught a glimpse at the same time of our little body from the parlour, huddled by the corner of the bar. The presence of so many witnesses decided him at once to flee. He crouched together, brushing on the wainscot, and made a dart like a serpent, striking for the door. But his tribulation was not yet entirely at an end, for even as he was passing Fettes clutched him by the arm and these words came in a whisper, and yet painfully distinct, "Have you seen it again?"

The great rich London doctor cried out aloud with a sharp, throttling cry; he dashed his questioner across the open space, and, with his hands over his head, fled out of the door like a detected thief. Before it had occurred to one of us to make a movement, the fly was already rattling towards the station. The scene was over like a dream, but the dream had left proofs and traces of its passage. Next day the servant found the fine gold spectacles broken on the threshold, and that very night we were all standing breathless by the bar-room window, and Fettes at our side, sober, pale, and resolute in look.

"God protect us, Mr Fettes!" said the landlord, coming first into possession of his customary senses. "What in the universe is all this? These are strange things you have been saying."

Fettes turned towards us; he looked us each in succession in the face. "See if you can hold your tongues," said he. "That man Macfarlane is not safe to cross; those that have done so already have repented it too late."

And then, without so much as finishing his third glass, far less waiting for the other two, he bade us goodbye and went forth, under the lamp of the hotel, into the black night.

We three turned to our places in the parlour, with the big red fire and four clear candles; and as we recapitulated what had passed the first chill of our surprise soon changed into a glow of curiosity. We sat late; it was the latest session I have known in the old George. Each man, before we parted, had his theory that he was bound to prove; and none of us had any nearer business in this world than to track out the past of our condemned companion, and surprise the secret that he shared with the great London doctor. It was no great boast, but I believe that I was a better hand at worming out a story than either of my fellows at the George; and perhaps there is now no other man alive who could narrate to you the following foul and unnatural events.

In his young days Fettes studied medicine in the schools of Edinburgh. He had talent of a kind, the talent that picks up swiftly what it hears and readily retails it for its own. He worked little at home; but he was civil, attentive, and intelligent in the presence of his masters. They soon picked him out as a lad who listened closely and remembered well; nay, strange as it seemed to me when I first heard it, he was in those days well favoured, and pleased by his exterior. There was, at that period, a certain extramural teacher of anatomy, whom I shall here designate by the letter K. His name was subsequently too well known. The man who bore it skulked through the streets of Edinburgh in disguise, while the mob that applauded at the execution of Burke called loudly for the blood of his employer. But Mr K— was then at the top of his vogue; he enjoyed a popularity due partly to his own talent and address, partly to the incapacity of his rival, the university professor. The students, at least, swore by his name, and Fettes believed himself, and was believed by others, to have laid the foundations of success when he had acquired the favour of this meteorically famous man. Mr K— was a *bon vivant* as well as an accomplished teacher; he liked a sly allusion no less than a careful preparation. In both capacities Fettes enjoyed and deserved his notice, and by the second year of his attendance he held the half-regular position of second demonstrator or sub-assistant in his class.

In this capacity, the charge of the theatre and lecture room devolved in particular upon his shoulders. He had to answer for the cleanliness of the premises and the conduct of the other students, and it was a part of his duty to supply, receive, and divide the various subjects. It was with a view to this last—at that time very delicate—affair that he was lodged by Mr K— in the same wynd, and at last in the same building, with the dissecting room. Here, after a night of turbulent pleasures, his hand still tottering, his sight still misty and confused, he would be called out of bed in the black hours before the winter dawn by the unclean and desperate interlopers who supplied the table. He would open the door to these men, since infamous throughout the land. He would help them with their tragic burthen, pay them their sordid price, and remain alone, when they were gone, with the unfriendly relics of humanity. From such a scene he would return to snatch another hour or two of slumber, to repair the abuses of the night, and refresh himself for the labours of the day.

Few lads could have been more insensible to the impressions of a life thus passed among the ensigns of mortality. His mind was closed against all general considerations. He was incapable of interest in the fate and fortunes of another, the slave of his own desires and low ambitions. Cold, light and selfish in the last resort, he had that modicum of prudence, miscalled morality, which keeps a man from inconvenient drunkenness or punishable theft. He coveted, besides, a measure of consideration from his masters and his fellow-pupils, and he had no desire to fail conspicuously in the external parts of life. Thus he made it his pleasure to gain some distinction in his studies, and day after day rendered unimpeachable eye-service to his employer, Mr K——. For his day of work he indemnified himself by nights of roaring, blackguardly enjoyment; and when that balance had been struck, the organ that he called his conscience declared itself content.

The supply of subjects was a continual trouble to him as well as to his master. In that large and busy class, the raw material of the anatomists kept perpetually running out; and the business thus rendered necessary was not only unpleasant in itself, but threatened dangerous consequences to all who were concerned. It was the policy of Mr K—— to ask no questions in his dealings with the trade. "They bring the body, and we pay the price," he used to say, dwelling on the alliteration—"*quid pro quo*." And again, and somewhat profanely, "Ask no questions," he would tell his assistants, "for conscience' sake." There was no understanding that the subjects were provided by the crime of murder. Had that idea been broached to him in words, he would have recoiled in horror; but the lightness of his speech upon so grave a matter was, in itself, an offence against good manners, and a temptation to the men with whom he dealt. Fettes, for instance, had often remarked to himself upon the singular freshness of the bodies. He had been struck again and again by the hang-dog, abominable looks of the ruffians who came to him before the dawn; and, putting things together clearly in his private thoughts, he perhaps attributed a meaning too immoral and too categorical to the unguarded counsels of his master. He understood his duty, in short, to have three branches: to take what was brought, to pay the price, and to avert the eye from any evidence of crime.

One November morning this policy of silence was put sharply to the test. He had been awake all night with a racking toothache—pacing his room like a caged beast or throwing himself in fury on his bed—and had fallen at last into that profound, uneasy slumber that so often follows on a night of pain, when he was awakened by the third or fourth angry repetition of the concerted signal. There was a thin, bright moonshine: it was bitter cold, windy, and frosty; the town had not yet awakened, but an indefinable stir already preluded the noise and business of the day. The ghouls had come later than usual, and they seemed more than usually eager to be gone. Fettes, sick with sleep, lighted them upstairs. He heard their grumbling Irish voices through a dream; and as they stripped the sack from their sad merchandise he leaned dozing with his shoulder propped against the wall; he had to shake himself to find the men their money. As he did so his eyes lighted on the dead face. He started: he took two steps nearer, with the candle raised.

"God Almighty!" he cried. "That is Jane Galbraith!"

The men answered nothing, but they shuffled nearer the door.

"I know her, I tell you," he continued. "She was alive and hearty yesterday. It's impossible she can be dead; it's impossible you should have got this body fairly."

"Sure, sir, you're mistaken entirely," asserted one of the men.

But the other looked Fettes darkly in the eyes, and demanded the money on the spot.

It was impossible to misconceive the threat or to exaggerate the danger. The lad's heart failed him. He stammered some excuses, counted out the sum, and saw his hateful visitors depart. No sooner were they gone than he hastened to confirm his doubts. By a dozen unquestionable marks he identified the girl he had jested with the day before. He saw, with horror, marks upon her body that might well betoken violence. A panic seized him, and he took refuge in his room. There he reflected at length over the discovery that he had made; considered soberly the bearing of Mr K—'s instructions and the danger to himself of interference in so serious a business, and at last, in sore perplexity, determined to wait for the advice of his immediate superior, the class assistant.

This was a young doctor, Wolfe Macfarlane, a high favourite among all the restless students, clever, dissipated, and unscrupulous to the last degree. He had travelled and studied abroad. His manners were agreeable and a little forward. He was an authority on the stage, skilful on the ice or the links with skate or golf-club; he dressed with nice audacity, and to put the finishing touch upon his glory, he kept a gig and a strong trotting-horse. With Fettes he was on terms of intimacy; indeed their relative positions called for some community of life; and when subjects were scarce the pair would drive far into the country in Macfarlane's gig, visit and desecrate some lonely graveyard, and return before dawn with their booty to the door of the dissecting room.

On that particular morning Macfarlane arrived somewhat earlier than his wont. Fettes heard him, and met him on the stairs, told him his story, and showed him the cause of his alarm. Macfarlane examined the marks on her body.

"Yes," he said with a nod, "it looks fishy."

"Well, what should I do?" asked Fettes.

"Do?" repeated the other. "Do you want to do anything? Least said soonest mended, I should say."

"Someone else might recognize her," objected Fettes. "She was as well known as the Castle Rock."

"We'll hope not," said Macfarlane, "and if anybody does—well you didn't, don't you see, and there's an end. The fact is, this has been going on too long. Stir up the mud, and you'll get K— into the most unholy trouble; you'll be in a shocking box yourself. So will I, if you come to that. I should like to know how any one of us would look, or what the devil we should have to say for ourselves, in any Christian witness-box. For me, you know there's one thing certain—that, practically speaking, all our subjects have been murdered."

"Macfarlane!" cried Fettes.

"Come now!" sneered the other. "As if you hadn't suspected it yourself!"

"Suspecting is one thing—"

"And proof another. Yes, I know; and I'm as sorry as you are this should have come here," tapping the body with his cane. "The next best thing for me is not to recognize it; and," he added coolly, "I don't. You may, if you please. I don't dictate, but I think a man of the world would do as I do; and I may add, I fancy that is what K— would look for at our hands. The question is, why did he choose us two for his assistants? And I answer, because he didn't want old wives."

This was the tone of all others to affect the mind of a lad like Fettes. He agreed to imitate Macfarlane. The body of the unfortunate girl was duly dissected, and no one remarked or appeared to recognize her.

One afternoon, when his day's work was over, Fettes dropped into a popular tavern and found Macfarlane sitting with a stranger. This was a small man, very pale and dark, with coal-black eyes. The cut of his features gave a promise of intellect and refinement which was but feebly realized in his manners, for he proved, upon a nearer acquaintance, coarse, vulgar, and stupid. He exercised, however, a very remarkable control over Macfarlane; issued orders like the Great Bashaw; became inflamed at the least discussion or delay, and commented rudely on the servility with which he was obeyed. This most offensive person took a fancy to Fettes on the spot, plied him with drinks, and honoured him with unusual confidences on his past career. If a tenth part of what he confessed were true, he was a very loathsome rogue; and the lad's vanity was tickled by the attention of so experienced a man.

"I'm a pretty bad fellow myself," the stranger remarked, "but Macfarlane is the boy. Toddy Macfarlane I call him. Toddy, order your friend another glass." Or it might be, "Toddy, you jump up and shut the door." "Toddy hates me," he said again. "Oh, yes, Toddy, you do!"

"Don't call me that confounded name," growled Macfarlane.

"Hear him! Did you ever see the lads play knife? He would like to do that all over my body," remarked the stranger.

"We medicals have a better way than that," said Fettes. "When we dislike a dead friend of ours, we dissect him."

Macfarlane looked up sharply, as though this jest was scarcely to his mind.

The afternoon passed. Gray, for that was the stranger's name, invited Fettes to join them at dinner, ordered a feast so sumptuous that the tavern was thrown in commotion, and when all was done commanded Macfarlane to settle the bill. It was late before they separated; the man Gray was incapably drunk. Macfarlane, sobered by his fury, chewed the cud of the money he had been forced to squander and the slights he had been obliged to swallow. Fettes, with various liquors singing in his head, returned home with devious footsteps and a mind entirely in abeyance. Next day Macfarlane was absent from the class, and Fettes smiled to himself as he imagined him still squiring the intolerable Gray from tavern to tavern. As soon as the hour of liberty had struck he posted from place to place in quest of his last night's companions. He could find them, however, nowhere; so returned early to his rooms, went early to bed, and slept the sleep of the just.

At four in the morning he was awakened by the well known signal. Descending to the door, he was filled with astonishment to find Macfarlane with his gig, and in the gig one of those long and ghastly packages with which he was so well acquainted.

"What?" he cried. "Have you been out alone? How did you manage?"

But Macfarlane silenced him roughly, bidding him turn to business. When they had got the body upstairs and laid it on the table, Macfarlane made at first as if he were going away. Then he paused and seemed to hesitate; and then, "You had better look at the face," said he, in tones of some constraint. "You had better," he repeated, as Fettes only stared at him in wonder.

"But where, and how, and when did you come by it?" cried the other.

"Look at the face," was the only answer.

Fettes was staggered; strange doubts assailed him. He looked from the young doctor to the body, and then back again. At last, with a start, he did as he was bidden. He had almost expected the sight that met his eyes, and yet the shock was cruel. To see, fixed in the rigidity of death and naked on that coarse layer of sack-cloth, the man whom he had left well-clad and full of meat and sin upon the threshold of a tavern, awoke, even in the thoughtless Fettes, some of the terrors of the conscience. It was a *cras tibi* which re-echoed in his soul, that two whom he had known should have come to lie upon these icy tables. Yet these were only secondary thoughts. His first concern regarded Wolfe. Unprepared for a challenge so momentous, he knew not how to look his comrade in the face. He durst not meet his eye, and he had neither words nor voice at his command.

It was Macfarlane himself who made the first advance. He came up quietly behind and laid his hand gently but firmly on the other's shoulder.

"Richardson," said he, "may have the head."

Now Richardson was a student who had long been anxious for that portion of the human subject to dissect. There was no answer, and the murderer resumed: "Talking of business, you must pay me; your accounts, you see, must tally."

Fettes found a voice, the ghost of his own: "Pay you!" he cried. "Pay you for that?"

"Why, yes, of course you must. By all means and on every possible account, you must," returned the other. "I dare not give it for nothing, you dare not take it for nothing; it would compromise us both. This is another case like Jane Galbraith's. The more things are wrong the more we must act as if all were right. Where does old K— keep his money —"

"There," answered Fettes hoarsely, pointing to a cupboard in the corner.

"Give me the key, then," said the other, calmly, holding out his hand.

There was an instant's hesitation, and the die was cast. Macfarlane could not suppress a nervous twitch, the infinitesimal mark of an immense relief, as he felt the key turn between his fingers. He opened the cupboard, brought out pen and ink and a paper-book that stood in one compartment, and separated from the funds in a drawer a sum suitable to the occasion.

"Now, look here," he said, "there is the payment made—first proof of your good faith: first step to your security. You have now to clinch it by a second. Enter the payment in your book, and then you for your part may defy the devil."

The next few seconds were for Fettes an agony of thought; but in balancing his terrors it was the most immediate that triumphed. Any future difficulty seemed almost welcome if he could avoid a present quarrel with Macfarlane. He set down the candle which he had been carrying all the time, and with a steady hand entered the date, the nature, and the amount of the transaction.

"And now," said Macfarlane, "it's only fair that you should pocket the lucre. I've had my share already. By-the-by, when a man of the world falls into a bit of luck, he has a few shillings extra in his pocket—I'm ashamed to speak of it, but there's a rule of conduct in the case. No treating, no purchase of expensive class-books, no squaring of old debts; borrow, don't lend."

"Macfarlane," began Fettes, still somewhat hoarsely. "I have put my neck in a halter to oblige you."

"To oblige me?" cried Wolfe. "Oh, come! You did, as near as I can see the matter, what you downright had to do in self defence. Suppose I got into trouble, where would you be? This second little matter flows clearly from the first. Mr Gray is the continuation of Miss Galbraith. You can't begin and then stop. If you begin, you must keep on beginning; that's the truth. No rest for the wicked."

A horrible sense of blackness and the treachery of fate seized hold upon the soul of the unhappy student.

"My God!" he cried, "but what I have done? and when did I begin? To be made a class assistant—in the name of reason, where's the harm in that? Service wanted the position; Service might have got it. Would *he* have been where *I* am now?"

"My dear fellow," said Macfarlane, "what a boy you are! What harm *has* come to you? What harm *can* come to you if you hold your tongue? Why, man, do you know what this life is? There are two squads of us—the lions and the lambs. If you're a lamb, you'll come to lie upon these tables like Gray or Jane Galbraith; if you're a lion, you'll live and drive a horse like me, like K——, like all the world with any wit or courage. You're staggered at the first. But look at K——! My dear fellow, you're clever, you have pluck. I like you, and K—— likes you. You were born to lead the hunt: and I tell you, on my honour and my experience of life, three days from now you'll laugh at all these scarecrows like a high school boy at a farce."

And with that Macfarlane took his departure and drove off up the wynd in his gig to get under cover before daylight. Fettes was thus left alone with his regrets. He saw the miserable peril in which he stood involved. He saw, with inexpressible dismay, that there was no limit to his weakness, and that, from concession to concession, he had fallen from the arbiter of Macfarlane's destiny to his paid and helpless accomplice. He would have given the world to have been a little braver at the time, but it did not occur to him that he might still be brave.

The secret of Jane Galbraith and the cursed entry in the daybook closed his mouth.

Hours passed; the class began to arrive; the members of the unhappy Gray were dealt out to one and to another, and received without remark. Richardson was made happy with the head; and before the hour of freedom rang Fettes trembled with exultation to perceive how far they had already gone towards safety.

For two days he continued to watch, with increasing joy, the dreadful process of disguise.

On the third day Macfarlane made his appearance. He had been ill, he said; but he made up for lost time by the energy with which he directed the students. To Richardson in particular he extended the most valuable assistance and advice, and that student, encouraged by the praise of the demonstrator, burned high with ambitious hopes, and saw the medal already in his grasp.

Before the week was out Macfarlane's prophecy had been fulfilled. Fettes had outlived his terrors and had forgotten his baseness. He began to plume himself upon his courage, and had so arranged the story in his mind that he could look back on these events with an unhealthy pride. Of his accomplice he saw but little. They met, of course, in the business of the class; they received their orders together from Mr K——. At times they had a word or two in private, and Macfarlane was from first to last particularly kind and jovial. But it was plain that he avoided any reference to their common secret; and even when Fettes whispered to him that he had cast in his lot with the lions and forsworn the lambs, he only signed to him smilingly to hold his peace.

At length an occasion arose which drew the pair once more into a closer union. Mr K—— was again short of subjects; pupils were eager, and it was a part of this teacher's pretensions to be always well supplied. At the same time there came the news of a burial in the rustic graveyard of Glencorse. Time has little changed the place in question. It stood then, as now, upon the crossroad, out of call of human habitations, and buried fathoms deep in the foliage of six cedar trees. The cries of the sheep upon the neighbouring hills, the streamlets upon either hand, one loudly singing among pebbles, the other dripping furtively from pond to pond, the stir of the wind in mountainous old flowering chestnuts, and once in seven days the voice of the bell and the old tunes of the precentor, were the only sounds that disturbed the silence around the rural church. The Resurrection Man—to use a by-name of the period—was not to be deterred by any of the sanctities of customary piety. It was part of his trade to despise and desecrate the scrolls and trumpets of old tombs, the paths worn by the feet of

worshippers and mourners, and the offerings and the inscriptions of bereaved affection. To rustic neighbourhoods, where love is more than commonly tenacious, and where some bonds of blood or fellowship unite the entire society of a parish, the body-snatcher, far from being repelled by natural respect, was attracted by the ease and safety of the task. To bodies that had been laid in earth, in joyful expectation of a far different awakening, there came that hasty, lamp-lit, terror-haunted resurrection of the spade and mattock. The coffin was forced, the cerements torn, and the melancholy relics, clad in sackcloth, after being rattled for hours on moonless by-ways, were at length exposed to uttermost indignities before a class of gaping boys.

Somewhat as two vultures may swoop upon a dying lamb, Fettes and Macfarlane were to be let loose upon a grave in that green and quiet resting place. The wife of a farmer, a woman who had lived for sixty years, and been known for nothing but good butter and a godly conversation, was to be rooted from her grave at midnight and carried, dead and naked, to that far away city that she had always honoured with her Sunday best; the place beside her family was to be empty till the crack of doom; her innocent and almost venerable members to be exposed to that last curiosity of the anatomist.

Late one afternoon the pair set forth, well wrapped in cloaks and furnished with a formidable bottle. It rained without remission—a cold, dense, lashing rain. Now and again there blew a puff of wind, but these sheets of falling water kept it down. Bottle and all, it was a sad and silent drive as far as Penicuik, where they were to spend the evening. They stopped once, to hide their implements in a thick bush not far from the churchyard, and once again at the Fisher's Tryst, to have a toast before the kitchen fire and vary their nips of whisky with a glass of ale. When they reached their journey's end the gig was housed, the horse was fed and comforted, and the two young doctors in a private room sat down to the best dinner and the best wine the house afforded. The lights, the fire, the beating rain upon the window, the cold, incongruous work that lay before them, added zest to their enjoyment of the meal. With every glass their cordiality increased. Soon Macfarlane handed a little pile of gold to his companion.

"A compliment," he said. "Between friends these little damned accommodations ought to fly like pipe-lights."

Fettes pocketed the money, and applauded the sentiment to the echo. "You are a philosopher," he cried. "I was an ass till I knew you. You and K— between you, by the Lord Harry! but you'll make a man of me."

"Of course we shall," applauded Macfarlane. "A man? I tell you, it required a man to back me up the other morning. There are some big, brawling, forty-year-old cowards who would have turned sick at the look of the damned thing; but not you—you kept your head. I watched you."

"Well, and why not?" Fettes thus vaunted himself. "It was no affair of mine. There was nothing to gain on the one side but disturbance, and on the other I could count on your gratitude, don't you see?" And he slapped his pocket till the gold pieces rang.

Macfarlane somehow felt a certain touch of alarm at these unpleasant words. He may have regretted that he had taught his young companion so successfully, but he had no time to interfere, for the other noisily continued in this boastful strain:

"The great thing is not to be afraid. Now, between you and me, I don't want to hang—that's practical; but for all cant, Macfarlane, I was born with a contempt. Hell, God, Devil, right, wrong, sin, crime, and all the old gallery of curiosities—they may frighten boys, but men of the world, like you and me, despise them. Here's to the memory of Gray!"

It was by this time growing somewhat late. The gig, according to order, was brought round to the door with both lamps brightly shining, and the young men had to pay their bill and take the road. They announced that they were bound for Peebles, and drove in that direction till they were clear of the last houses of the town; then, extinguishing the lamps, returned upon their course, and followed a by-road towards Glencorse. There was no sound but that of their own passage, and the incessant, strident pouring of the rain. It was pitch dark; here and there a white gate or a white stone in the wall guided them for a short space across the night; but for the most part it was at a foot pace, and almost groping, that they picked their way through that resonant blackness to their solemn and isolated destination. In the sunken woods that traverse the neighbourhood of the burying ground the last glimmer failed them, and it became necessary to kindle a match and re-illumine one of the lanterns of the gig. Thus, under the dripping trees, and environed by huge and moving shadows, they reached the scene of their unhallowed labours.

They were both experienced in such affairs, and powerful with the spade; and they had scarce been twenty minutes at their task before they were rewarded by a dull rattle on the coffin lid. At the same moment Macfarlane, having hurt his hand upon a stone, flung it carelessly above his head. The grave, in which they now stood almost to the shoulders, was close to the edge of the plateau of the graveyard; and the gig lamp had been propped, the better to illuminate their labours, against a tree, and on the immediate verge of the steep bank descending to the stream. Chance had taken a sure aim with the stone. Then came a clang of broken glass; night fell upon them; sounds alternately dull and ringing announced the bounding of the lantern down the bank, and its occasional collision with the trees. A stone or two, which it had dislodged in its descent rattled behind it into the profundities of the glen; and then silence, like night, resumed its sway; and they might bend their hearing to its utmost pitch, but naught was to be heard except the rain, now marching to the wind, now steadily falling over miles of open country.

They were so nearly at an end of their abhorred task that they judged it wisest to complete it in the dark. The coffin was exhumed and broken open; the body inserted in the dripping sack and carried between them to the gig; one mounted to keep it in its place, and the other, taking the horse by the mouth, groped along by the wall and bush until they reached the wider road by the Fisher's Tryst. Here was a faint disused radiancy, which they hailed like daylight; by that they pushed the horse to a good pace and began to rattle along merrily in the direction of the town.

They had both been wetted to the skin during their operations, and now, as the gig jumped among the deep ruts, the thing that stood propped between them fell now upon one and now upon the other. At every repetition of the horrid contact each instinctively repelled it with greater haste; and the process, natural although it was, began to tell upon the nerves of the companions. Macfarlane made some ill-favoured jest about the farmer's wife, but it came hollowly from his lips, and was allowed to drop in silence. Still their unnatural burthen bumped from side to side; and now the head would be laid, as if in confidence, upon their shoulders, and now the drenching sackcloth would flap icily about their faces. A creeping chill began to possess the soul of Fettes. He peered at the bundle, and it seemed somehow larger than at first. All over the countryside, and from every degree of distance, the farm dogs accompanied their passage with tragic ululations; and it grew and grew upon his mind that some unnatural miracle had been achieved, that some nameless change had befallen the dead body, and that it was in fear of their unholy burthen that the dogs were howling.

"For God's sake," said he, making a great effort to arrive at speech, "for God's sake, let's have a light!"

Seemingly Macfarlane was affected in the same direction: for though he made no reply, he stopped the horse, passed the reins to his companion, got down, and proceeded to kindle the remaining lamp. They had by that time got no farther than the crossroad down to Auchendinny. The rain still poured as though the deluge were returning, and it was no easy matter to make a light in such a world of wet and darkness. When at last the flickering blue flame had been transferred to the wick and began to expand and clarify, and shed a wide circle of misty brightness round the gig, it became possible for the two young men to see each other and the thing they had along with them. The rain had moulded the rough sacking to the outlines of the body underneath; the head was distinct from the trunk, the shoulders plainly modelled: something at once spectral and human riveted their eyes upon the ghastly comrade of their drive.

For some time Macfarlane stood motionless, holding up the lamp. A nameless dread was swathed, like a wet sheet, about the body, and tightened the white skin upon the face of Fettes; a fear that was meaningless, a horror of what could not be, kept mounting to his brain. Another beat of the watch, and he had spoken. But his comrade forestalled him.

"That is not a woman," said Macfarlane, in a hushed voice.

"It was a woman when we put her in," whispered Fettes.

"Hold that lamp," said the other. "I must see her face."

And as Fettes took the lamp his companion untied the fastenings of the sack and drew down the cover from the head. The light fell very clear upon the dark, well-moulded features and smooth-shaven cheeks of a too familiar countenance, often beheld in dreams of both of these young men. A wild yell rang up into the night; each leaped from his own side into the roadway; the lamp fell, broke, and was extinguished; and the horse, terrified by this unusual commotion, bounded and went off towards Edinburgh at a gallop, bearing along with it, sole occupant of the gig, the body of the dead and long-dissected Gray.

# A Ghost Story

*Mark Twain*

I took a large room, far up Broadway, in a huge old building whose upper stories had been wholly unoccupied for years until I came. The place had long been given up to dust and cobwebs, to solitude and silence. I seemed groping among the tombs and invading the privacy of the dead, that first night I climbed up to my quarters. For the first time in my life a superstitious dread came over me; and as I turned a dark angle of the stairway and an invisible cobweb swung its slazy woof in my face and clung there, I shuddered as one who had encountered a phantom.

I was glad enough when I reached my room and locked out the mold and the darkness. A cheery fire was burning in the grate, and I sat down before it with a comforting sense of relief. For two hours I sat there, thinking of bygone times; recalling old scenes, and summoning half-forgotten faces out of the mists of the past; listening, in fancy, to voices that long ago grew silent for all time, and to once familiar songs that nobody sings now. And as my reverie softened down to a sadder and sadder pathos, the shrieking of the winds outside softened to a wail, the angry beating of the rain against the panes diminished to a tranquil patter, and one by one the noises in the street subsided, until the hurrying footsteps of the last belated straggler died away in the distance and left no sound behind.

The fire had burned low. A sense of loneliness crept over me. I arose and undressed, moving on tiptoe about the room, doing stealthily what I had to do, as if I were environed by sleeping enemies whose slumbers it would be fatal to break. I covered up in bed, and lay listening to the rain and wind and the faint creaking of distant shutters, till they lulled me to sleep.

I slept profoundly, but how long I do not know. All at once I found myself awake, and filled with a shuddering expectancy. All was still. All but my own heart—I could hear it beat. Presently the bedclothes began to slip away slowly toward the foot of the bed, as if some one were pulling them! I could not stir; I could not speak. Still the blankets slipped deliberately away, till my breast was uncovered. Then with a great effort I seized them and drew them over my head. I waited, listened, waited. Once more that steady pull began, and once more I lay torpid a century of dragging seconds till my breast was naked again. At last I roused my energies and snatched the covers back to their place and held them with a strong grip. I waited. By and by I felt a faint tug, and took a fresh grip. The tug strengthened to a steady strain—it grew stronger and stronger. My hold parted, and for the third time the blanket slid away. I groaned. An answering groan came from the foot of the bed! Beaded drops of sweat stood upon my forehead. I was more dead than alive. Presently I heard a heavy footstep in my room—the step of an elephant, it seemed to me—it was not like anything human. But it was moving *from* me—there was relief in that. I heard it approach the door—pass out without moving bolt or lock—and wander away among the dismal corridors, straining the floors and joists till they creaked again as it passed—and then silence reigned once more.

When my excitement had calmed, I said to myself, "This is a dream—simply a hideous dream." And so I lay thinking it over until I convinced myself that it *was* a dream, and then a comforting laugh relaxed my lips and I was happy again. I got up and struck a light;

and when I found that the locks and bolts were just as I had left them, another soothing laugh welled in my heart and rippled from my lips. I took my pipe and lit it, and was just sitting down before the fire, when—down went the pipe out of my nerveless fingers, the blood forsook my cheeks, and my placid breathing was cut short with a gasp! In the ashes on the hearth, side by side with my own bare footprint, was another, so vast that in comparison mine was by an infant's! Then I had ***had*** a visitor, and the elephant tread was explained.

I put out the light and returned to bed, palsied with fear. I lay a long time, peering into the darkness, and listening. Then I heard a grating noise overhead, like the dragging of a heavy body across the floor; then the throwing down of the body, and the shaking of my windows in response to the concussion. In distant parts of the building I heard the muffled slamming of doors. I heard, at intervals, stealthy footsteps creeping in and out among the corridors, and up and down the stairs. Sometimes these noises approached my door, hesitated, and went away again. I heard the clanking of chains faintly, in remote passages, and listened while the clanking grew nearer—while it wearily climbed the stairways, marking each move by the loose surplus of chain that fell with an accented rattle upon each succeeding step as the goblin that bore it advanced. I heard muttered sentences; half-uttered screams that seemed smothered violently; and the swish of invisible garments, the rush of invisible wings. Then I became conscious that my chamber was invaded—that I was not alone. I heard sighs and breathings about my bed, and mysterious whisperings. Three little spheres of soft phosphorescent light appeared on the ceiling directly over my head, clung and glowed there a moment, and then dropped—two of them upon my face and one upon the pillow. They spattered, liquidly, and felt warm. Intuition told me they had turned to gouts of blood as they fell—I needed no light to satisfy myself of that. Then I saw pallid faces, dimly luminous, and white uplifted hands, floating bodiless in the air—floating a moment and then disappearing. The whispering ceased, and the voices and the sounds, and a solemn stillness followed. I waited and listened. I felt that I must have light or die. I was weak with fear. I slowly raised myself toward a sitting posture, and my face came in contact with a clammy hand! All strength went from me apparently, and I fell back like a stricken invalid. Then I heard the rustle of a garment—it seemed to pass to the door and go out.

When everything was still once more, I crept out of bed, sick and feeble, and lit the gas with a hand that trembled as if it were aged with a hundred years. The light brought some little cheer to my spirits. I sat down and fell into a dreamy contemplation of that great footprint in the ashes. By and by its outlines began to waver and grow dim. I glanced up and the broad gas-flame was slowly wilting away. In the same moment I heard that elephantine tread again. I noted its approach, nearer and nearer, along the musty halls, and dimmer and dimmer the light waned. The tread reached my very door and paused—the light had dwindled to a sickly blue, and all things about me lay in a spectral twilight. The door did not open, and yet I felt a faint gust of air fan my cheek, and presently was conscious of a huge, cloudy presence before me. I watched it with fascinated eyes. A pale glow stole over the Thing; gradually its cloudy folds took shape—an arm appeared, then legs, then a body, and last a great sad face looked out of the vapor. Stripped of its filmy housings, naked, muscular and comely, the majestic Cardiff Giant loomed above me!

All my misery vanished—for a child might know that no harm could come with that benignant countenance. My cheerful spirits returned at once, and in sympathy with them the gas flamed up brightly again. Never a lonely outcast was so glad to welcome company as I was to greet the friendly giant. I said:

"Why, is it nobody but you? Do you know, I have been scared to death for the last two or three hours? I am most honestly glad to see you. I wish I had a chair—Here, here, don't try to sit down in that thing!"

But it was too late. He was in it before I could stop him, and down he went—I never saw a chair shivered so in my life.

"Stop, stop, you'll ruin ev—"

Too late again. There was another crash, and another chair was resolved into its original elements.

"Confound it, haven't you got any judgment at all? Do you want to ruin all the furniture on the place? Here, here, you petrified fool—"

But it was no use. Before I could arrest him he had sat down on the bed, and it was a melancholy ruin.

"Now what sort of a way is that to do? First you come lumbering about the place bringing a legion of vagabond goblins along with you to worry me to death, and then when I overlook an indelicacy of costume which would not be tolerated anywhere by cultivated people except in a respectable theater, and not even there if the nudity were of *your* sex, you repay me by wrecking all the furniture you can find to sit down on. And why will you? You damage yourself as much as you do me. You have broken off the end of your spinal column, and littered up the floor with chips of your hams till the place looks like a marble yard. You ought to be ashamed of yourself—you are big enough to know better."

"Well, I will not break any more furniture. But what am I to do? I have not had a chance to sit down for a century." And the tears came into his eyes.

"Poor devil," I said, "I should not have been so harsh with you. And you are an orphan, too, no doubt. But sit down on the floor here—nothing else can stand your weight—and besides, we cannot be sociable with you away up there above me; I want you down where I can perch on this high counting-house stool and gossip with you face to face."

So he sat down on the floor, and lit a pipe which I gave him, threw one of my red blanket over his shoulders, inverted my sitz-bath on his head, helmet fashion, and made himself picturesque and comfortable. Then he crossed his ankles, while I renewed the fire, and exposed the flat, honeycombed bottoms of his prodigious feet to the grateful warmth.

"What is the matter with the bottom of your feet and the back of your legs, that they are gouged up so?"

"Infernal chilblains—I caught them clear up to the back of my head, roosting out there under Newell's farm. But I love the place; I love it as one loves his old home. There is no peace for me like the peace I feel when I am there."

We talked along for half an hour, and then I noticed that he looked tired, and spoke of it.

"Tired?" he said. "Well, I should think so. And now I will tell you all about it, since you have treated me so well. I am the spirit of the Petrified Man that lies across the street there in the museum. I am the ghost of the Cardiff Giant. I can have no rest, no peace, till they have given that poor body burial again. Now what was the most natural thing for me to do, to make men satisfy this wish? Terrify them into it!—haunt the place where the body lay! So I haunted the museum night after night. I even got other spirits to help me. But it did no good, for nobody ever came to the museum at midnight. Then it occurred to me to come over the way and haunt this place a little. I felt that if I ever got a hearing I must succeed, for I had the most efficient company that perdition could furnish. Night after night we have shivered around through these mildewed halls, dragging chains, groaning, whispering, tramping up and down stairs, till, to tell you the truth, I am almost worn out. But when I saw a light in your room to-night I roused my energies again and went at it with a deal of the old freshness. But I am tired out—entirely fagged out. Give me, I beseech you, give me some hope!"

I lit off my perch in a burst of excitement, and exclaimed:

"This transcends everything! everything that ever did occur! Why you poor blundering old fossil, you have had all your trouble for nothing—you have been haunting a *plaster cast* of yourself—the real Cardiff Giant is in Albany![1] Confound it, don't you know your own remains?"

I never saw such a eloquent look of shame, of pitiable humiliation, overspread a countenance before.

The Petrified Man rose slowly to his feet, and said:

"Honestly, *is* that true?"

"As true as I am sitting here."

He took the pipe from his mouth and laid it on the mantel, then stood irresolute a moment (unconsciously, from old habit, thrusting his hands where his pantaloons pockets should have been, and meditatively dropping his chin on his breast), and finally said:

"Well—I *never* felt so absurd before. The Petrified Man has sold everybody else, and now the mean fraud has ended by selling its own ghost! My son, if there is any charity left in your heart for a poor friendless phantom like me, don't let this get out. Think how *you* would feel if you had made such an ass of yourself."

I heard his stately tramp die away, step by step down the stairs and out into the deserted street, and felt sorry that he was gone, poor fellow—and sorrier still that he had carried off my red blanket and my bathtub.

---

A fact. The original fraud was ingeniously and fraudfully duplicated, and exhibited in New York as the "only genuine" Cardiff Giant (to the unspeakable disgust of the owners of the real colossus) at the very same time that the latter was drawing crowds at a museum in Albany.

# DRACULA'S GUEST

*Bram Stoker*

This independent tale by Bram Stoker was intended to be worked into his famous novel *Dracula*. In fact, it was remoulded as the following short story and was first published in a posthumous collection of Stoker's horror tales.

When we started for our drive the sun was shining brightly on Munich, and the air was full of the joyousness of early summer. Just as we were about to depart, Herr Delbrück (the maitre d'hôtel of the Quatre Saisons, where I was staying) came down, bareheaded, to the carriage and, after wishing me a pleasant drive, said to the coachman, still holding his hand on the handle of the carriage door:

"Remember you are back by nightfall. The sky looks bright but there is a shiver in the north wind that says there may be a sudden storm. But I am sure you will not be late." Here he smiled, and added, "for you know what night it is."

Johann answered with an emphatic, "Ja, mein Herr," and, touching his hat, drove off quickly. When we had cleared the town, I said, after signalling to him to stop:

"Tell me, Johann, what is tonight?"

He crossed himself, as he answered laconically: "Walpurgis nacht." Then he took out his watch, a great, old-fashioned German silver thing as big as a turnip, and looked at it, with his eyebrows gathered together and a little impatient shrug of his shoulders. I realized that this was his way of respectfully protesting against the unnecessary delay, and sank back in the carriage, merely motioning him to proceed. He started off rapidly, as if to make up for lost time. Every now and then the horses seemed to throw up their heads and sniffed the air suspiciously. On such occasions I often looked round in alarm. The road was pretty bleak, for we were traversing a sort of high, wind-swept plateau. As we drove, I saw a road that looked but little used, and which seemed to dip through a little, winding valley. It looked so inviting that, even at the risk of offending him, I called Johann to stop—and when he had pulled up, I told him I would like to drive down that road. He made all sorts of excuses, and frequently crossed himself as he spoke. This somewhat piqued my curiosity, so I asked him various questions. He answered fencingly, and repeatedly looked at his watch in protest. Finally I said:

"Well, Johann, I want to go down this road. I shall not ask you to come unless you like; but tell me why you do not like to go, that is all I ask." For answer he seemed to throw himself off the box, so quickly did he reach the ground. Then he stretched out his hands appealingly to me, and implored me not to go. There was just enough of English mixed with the German for me to understand the drift of his talk. He seemed always just about to tell me something—the very idea of which evidently frightened him; but each time he pulled himself up, saying, as he crossed himself: "Walpurgis nacht!"

I tried to argue with him, but it was difficult to argue with a man when I did not know his language. The advantage certainly rested with him, for although he began to speak in English, of a very crude and broken kind, he always got excited and broke into his native tongue—and every time he did so, he looked at his watch. Then the horses became restless and sniffed the air. At this he grew very pale, and, looking around in a frightened way, he suddenly jumped forward, took them by the bridles and led them on some twenty feet. I followed, and asked why he had done this. For answer he crossed himself, pointed to the spot we had left and drew his carriage in the direction of the other road, indicating a cross, and said, first in German, then in English: "Buried him—him what killed themselves."

I remembered the old custom of burying suicides at cross-roads: "Ah! I see, a suicide. How interesting!" But for the life of me I could not make out why the horses were frightened.

Whilst we were talking, we heard a sort of sound between a yelp and a bark. It was far away; but the horses got very restless, and it took Johann all his time to quiet them. He was pale, and said: "It sounds like a wolf—but yet there are no wolves here now."

"No?" I said, questioning him; "isn't it long since the wolves were so near the city?"

"Long, long," he answered, "in the spring and summer; but with the snow the wolves have been here not so long."

Whilst he was petting the horses and trying to quiet them, dark clouds drifted rapidly across the sky. The sunshine passed away, and a breath of cold wind seemed to drift past us. It was only a breath, however, and more in the nature of a warning than a fact, for the sun came out brightly again. Johann looked under his lifted hand at the horizon and said:

"The storm of snow, he comes before long time." Then he looked at his watch again, and, straightway holding his reins firmly—for the horses were still pawing the ground restlessly and shaking their heads—he climbed to his box as though the time had come for proceeding on our journey.

I felt a little obstinate and did not at once get into the carriage.

"Tell me," I said, "about this place where the road leads," and I pointed down.

Again he crossed himself and mumbled a prayer, before he answered: "It is unholy."

"What is unholy?" I enquired.

"The village."

"Then there is a village?"

"No, no. No one lives there hundreds of years." My curiosity was piqued: "But you said there was a village."

"There was."

"Where is it now?"

Whereupon he burst out into a long story in German and English, so mixed up that I could not quite understand exactly what he said, but roughly I gathered that long ago, hundreds of years, men had died there and been buried in their graves; and sounds were heard under the clay, and when the graves were opened, men and women were found rosy with life and their mouths red with blood. And so, in haste to save their lives (aye, and their souls!—and here he crossed himself) those who were left fled away to other places, where the living lived, and the dead were dead and not—not something. He was evidently afraid to speak the last words. As he proceeded with his narration, he grew more and more excited. It seemed as if his imagination had got hold of him, and he ended in a perfect paroxysm of fear—white-faced, perspiring, trembling and looking round him, as if expecting that some dreadful presence would manifest itself there in the bright sunshine on the open plain. Finally, in an agony of desperation, he cried:

"Walpurgis nacht!" and pointed to the carriage for me to get in. All my English blood rose at this, and, standing back, I said:

"You are afraid, Johann—you are afraid. Go home; I shall return alone; the walk will do me good." The carriage door was open. I took from the seat my oak walking-stick—which I always carry on my holiday excursions—and closed the door, pointing back to Munich, and said, "Go home, Johann—Walpurgis nacht doesn't concern Englishmen."

The horses were now more restless than ever, and Johann was trying to hold them in, while excitedly imploring me not to do anything so foolish. I pitied the poor fellow, he was so deeply in earnest; but all the same I could not help laughing. His English was quite gone now. In his anxiety he had forgotten that his only means of making me understand was to talk my language, so he jabbered away in his native German. It began to be a little tedious. After giving the direction, "Home!" I turned to go down the cross-road into the valley.

With a despairing gesture, Johann turned his horses towards Munich. I leaned on my stick and looked after him. He went slowly along the road for a while: then there came over the crest of the hill a man tall and thin. I could see so much in the distance. When he drew near the horses, they began to jump and kick about, then to scream with terror. Johann could not hold them in; they bolted down the road, running away madly. I watched them out of sight, then looked for the stranger, but I found that he, too, was gone.

With a light heart I turned down the side road through the deepening valley to which Johann had objected. There was not the slightest reason, that I could see, for his objection; and I daresay I tramped for a couple of hours without thinking of time or distance, and certainly without seeing a person or a house. So far as the place was concerned, it was desolation itself. But I did not notice this particularly till, on turning a bend in the road, I came upon a scattered fringe of wood; then I recognized that I had been impressed unconsciously by the desolation of the region through which I had passed.

I sat down to rest myself, and began to look around. It struck me that it was considerably colder than it had been at the commencement of my walk—a sort of sighing sound seemed to be around me, with, now and then, high overhead, a sort of muffled roar. Looking upwards

I noticed that great thick clouds were drifting rapidly across the sky from North to South at a great height. There were signs of coming storm in some lofty stratum of the air. I was a little chilly, and, thinking that it was the sitting still after the exercise of walking, I resumed my journey.

The ground I passed over was now much more picturesque. There were no striking objects that the eye might single out; but in all there was a charm of beauty. I took little heed of time and it was only when the deepening twilight forced itself upon me that I began to think of how I should find my way home. The brightness of the day had gone. The air was cold, and the drifting of clouds high overhead was more marked. They were accompanied by a sort of far-away rushing sound, through which seemed to come at intervals that mysterious cry which the driver had said came from a wolf. For a while I hesitated. I had said I would see the deserted village, so on I went, and presently came on a wide stretch of open country, shut in by hills all around. Their sides were covered with trees which spread down to the plain, dotting, in clumps, the gentler slopes and hollows which showed here and there. I followed with my eye the winding of the road, and saw that it curved close to one of the densest of these clumps and was lost behind it.

As I looked there came a cold shiver in the air, and the snow began to fall. I thought of the miles and miles of bleak country I had passed, and then hurried on to seek the shelter of the wood in front. Darker and darker grew the sky, and faster and heavier fell the snow, till the earth before and around me was a glistening white carpet the further edge of which was lost in misty vagueness. The road was here but crude, and when on the level its boundaries were not so marked, as when it passed through the cuttings; and in a little while I found that I must have strayed from it, for I missed underfoot the hard surface, and my feet sank deeper in the grass and moss. Then the wind grew stronger and blew with ever increasing force, till I was fain to run before it. The air became icy-cold, and in spite of my exercise I began to suffer. The snow was now falling so thickly and whirling around me in such rapid eddies that I could hardly keep my eyes open. Every now and then the heavens were torn asunder by vivid lightning, and in the flashes I could see ahead of me a great mass of trees, chiefly yew and cypress all heavily coated with snow.

I was soon amongst the shelter of the trees, and there, in comparative silence, I could hear the rush of the wind high overhead. Presently the blackness of the storm had become merged in the darkness of the night. By-and-by the storm seemed to be passing away: it now only came in fierce puffs or blasts. At such moments the weird sound of the wolf appeared to be echoed by many similar sounds around me.

Now and again, through the black mass of drifting cloud, came a straggling ray of moonlight, which lit up the expanse, and showed me that I was at the edge of a dense mass of cypress and yew trees. As the snow had ceased to fall, I walked out from that shelter and began to investigate more closely. It appeared to me that, amongst so many old foundations as I had passed, there might be still standing a house in which, though in ruins, I could find some sort of shelter for a while. As I skirted the edge of the copse, I found that a low wall encircled it, and following this I presently found an opening. Here the cypresses formed an alley leading up to a square mass of some kind of building. Just as I caught sight of this, however, the drifting clouds obscured the moon, and I passed up the path in darkness. The wind must have grown colder, for I felt myself shiver as I walked; but there was hope of shelter, and I groped my way blindly on.

I stopped, for there was a sudden stillness. The storm had passed; and, perhaps in sympathy with nature's silence, my heart seemed to cease to beat. But this was only momentarily; for suddenly the moonlight broke through the clouds, showing me that I was in a graveyard, and that the square object before me was a great massive tomb of marble, as white as the snow that lay on and all around it. With the moonlight there came a fierce sigh of the storm, which appeared to resume its course with a long, low howl, as of many dogs or wolves. I was awed and shocked, and felt the cold perceptibly grow upon me till it seemed to grip me by the heart. Then while the flood of moonlight still fell on the marble tomb the storm gave further evidence of renewing, as though it was returning on its track. Impelled by some sort of fascination, I approached the sepulchre to see what it was, and why such a thing stood alone in such a place. I walked around it, and read, over the Doric door, in German—

COUNTESS DOLINGEN OF GRATZ
IN STYRIA
SOUGHT AND FOUND DEATH
1801.

On the top of the tomb, seemingly driven through the solid marble—for the structure was composed of a few vast blocks of stone—was a great iron spike or stake. On going to the back I saw, graven in great Russian letters:

The dead travel fast.

There was something so weird and uncanny about the whole thing that it gave me a turn and made me feel quite faint. I began to wish, for the first time, that I had taken Johann's advice. Here a thought struck me, which came under almost mysterious circumstances and with a terrible shock. This was Walpurgis Night!

Walpurgis Night, when, according to the belief of millions of people, the devil was abroad—when the graves were opened and the dead came forth and walked. When all evil things of earth and air and water held revel. This very place the driver had specially shunned. This was the depopulated village of centuries ago. This was where the suicide lay; and this was the place where I was alone—unmanned, shivering with cold in a shroud of snow with a wild storm gathering again upon me! It took all my philosophy, all the religion I have been taught, all my courage, not to collapse in a paroxysm of fright.

And now a perfect tornado burst upon me. The ground shook as though thousands of horses thundered across it; and this time the storm bore on its icy wings, not snow, but great hailstones which drove with such violence that they might have come from the thongs of Balearic slingers—hailstones that beat down leaf and branch and made the shelter of the cypresses of no more avail than though their stems were standing-corn. At the first I rushed to the nearest tree; but I was soon fain to leave it and seek the only spot that seemed to afford refuge, the deep Doric doorway of the marble tomb. There, crouching against the massive bronze-door, I gained a certain amount of protection from the beating of the hailstones, for now they only drove against me as they ricochetted from the ground and the side of the marble.

As I leaned against the door, it moved slightly and opened inwards. The shelter of even a tomb was welcome in that pitiless tempest, and I was about to enter it when there came a flash of forked lightning that lit up the whole expanse of the heavens. In the instant, as I am a living man, I saw, as my eyes were turned into the darkness of the tomb, a beautiful woman, with rounded cheeks and red lips, seemingly asleep on a bier. As the thunder broke overhead, I was grasped as by the hand of a giant and hurled out into the storm. The whole thing was so sudden that, before I could realize the shock, moral as well as physical, I found the hailstones beating me down. At the same time I had a strange, dominating feeling that I was not alone. I looked towards the tomb. Just then there came another blinding flash, which seemed to strike the iron stake that surmounted the tomb and to pour through to the earth, blasting and crumbling the marble, as in a burst of flame. The dead woman rose for a moment of agony, while she was lapped in the flame, and her bitter scream of pain was drowned in the thundercrash. The last thing I heard was this mingling of dreadful sound, as again I was seized in the giant-grasp and dragged away, while the hailstones beat on me, and the air around seemed reverberant with the howling of wolves. The last sight that I remembered was a vague, white, moving mass, as if all the graves around me had sent out the phantoms of their sheeted-dead, and that they were closing in on me through the white cloudiness of the driving hail.

Gradually there came a sort of vague beginning of consciousness; then a sense of weariness that was dreadful. For a time I remembered nothing; but slowly my senses returned. My feet seemed positively racked with pain, yet I could not move them. They seemed to be numbed. There was an icy feeling at the back of my neck and all down my spine, and my ears, like my feet, were dead, yet in torment; but there was in my breast a sense of warmth which was, by comparison, delicious. It was as a nightmare—a physical nightmare, if one may use such an expression; for some heavy weight on my chest made it difficult for me to breathe.

This period of semi-lethargy seemed to remain a long time, and as it faded away I must have slept or swooned. Then came a sort of loathing, like the first stage of sea-sickness, and a wild desire to be free from something—I knew not what. A vast stillness enveloped me as though all the world were asleep or dead—only broken by the low panting as of some animal close to me. I felt a warm rasping at my throat, then came a consciousness of the awful truth, which chilled me to the heart and sent the blood surging up through my brain. Some great animal was lying on me and now licking my throat. I feared to stir, for some instinct of prudence bade me lie still; but the brute seemed to realize that there was now some change in me, for it raised its head. Through my eyelashes I saw above me the two great flaming eyes of a gigantic wolf. Its sharp white teeth gleamed in the gaping red mouth, and I could feel its hot breath fierce and acrid upon me.

For another spell of time I remembered no more. Then I became conscious of a low growl, followed by a yelp, renewed again and again. Then, seemingly very far away, I heard a "Holloa! holloa!" as of many voices calling in unison. Cautiously I raised my head and looked in the direction whence the sound came; but the cemetery blocked my view. The wolf still continued to yelp in a strange way, and a red glare began to move round the grove of cypresses, as though following the sound. As the voices drew closer, the wolf yelped faster and louder. I feared to make either sound or motion. Nearer came the red glow, over the white pall which stretched into the darkness around me. Then all at once from beyond the trees there came at a trot a troop of horsemen bearing torches. The wolf rose from my breast and made for the cemetery. I saw one of the horsemen (soldiers by the caps and their long military cloaks) raise his carbine and take aim. A companion knocked up his arm, and I heard the ball whizz over my head. He had evidently taken my body for that of the wolf. Another sighted the animal as it slunk away, and a shot followed. Then, at a gallop, the troop rode forward—some towards me, others following the wolf as it disappeared amongst the snow-clad cypresses.

As they drew nearer I tried to move, but was powerless, although I could see and hear all that went on around me. Two or three of the soldiers jumped from their horses and knelt beside me. One of them raised my head, and placed his hand over my heart.

"Good news, comrades!" he cried. "His heart still beats!"

Then some brandy was poured down my throat; it put vigour into me, and I was able to open my eyes fully and look around. Lights and shadows were moving among the trees, and I heard men call to one another. They drew together, uttering frightened exclamations; and the lights flashed as the others came pouring out of the cemetery pell-mell, like men possessed. When the further ones came close to us, those who were around me asked them eagerly:

"Well, have you found him?"

The reply rang out hurriedly:

"No! no! Come away quick—quick! This is no place to stay, and on this of all nights!"

"What was it?" was the question, asked in all manner of keys. The answer came variously and all indefinitely as though the men were moved by some common impulse to speak, yet were restrained by some common fear from giving their thoughts.

"It—it—indeed!" gibbered one, whose wits had plainly given out for the moment.

"A wolf—and yet not a wolf!" another put in shudderingly.

"No use trying for him without the sacred bullet," a third remarked in a more ordinary manner.

"Serve us right for coming out on this night! Truly we have earned our thousand marks!" were the ejaculations of a fourth.

"There was blood on the broken marble," another said after a pause—"the lightning never brought that there. And for him—is he safe? Look at his throat! See, comrades, the wolf has been lying on him and keeping his blood warm."

The officer looked at my throat and replied:

"He is all right; the skin is not pierced. What does it all mean? We should never have found him but for the yelping of the wolf."

"What became of it?" asked the man who was holding up my head, and who seemed the least panic-stricken of the party, for his hands were steady and without tremor. On his sleeve was the chevron of a petty officer.

"It went to its home," answered the man, whose long face was pallid, and who actually shook with terror as he glanced around him fearfully. "There are graves enough there in which it may lie. Come, comrades—come quickly! Let us leave this cursed spot."

The officer raised me to a sitting posture, as he uttered a word of command; then several men placed me upon a horse. He sprang to the saddle behind me, took me in his arms, gave the word to advance; and, turning our faces away from the cypresses, we rode away in swift, military order.

As yet my tongue refused its office, and I was perforce silent. I must have fallen asleep; for the next thing I remembered was finding myself standing up, supported by a soldier on each side of me. It was almost broad daylight, and to the north a red streak of sunlight was reflected, like a path of blood, over the waste of snow. The officer was telling the men to say nothing of what they had seen, except that they found an English stranger, guarded by a large dog.

"Dog! that was no dog," cut in the man who had exhibited such fear. "I think I know a wolf when I see one."

The young officer answered calmly: "I said a dog."

"Dog!" reiterated the other ironically. It was evident that his courage was rising with the sun; and, pointing to me, he said, "Look at his throat. Is that the work of a dog, master?"

Instinctively I raised my hand to my throat, and as I touched it I cried out in pain. The men crowded round to look, some stooping down from their saddles; and again there came the calm voice of the young officer:

"A dog, as I said. If aught else were said we should only be laughed at."

I was then mounted behind a trooper, and we rode on into the suburbs on Munich. Here we came across a stray carriage, into which I was lifted, and it was driven off to the Quatre Saisons—the young officer accompanying me, whilst a trooper followed with his horse, and the others rode off to their barracks.

When we arrived, Herr Delbrück rushed so quickly down the steps to meet me, that it was apparent he had been watching within. Taking me by both hands he solicitously led me in. The officer saluted me and was turning to withdraw, when I recognized his purpose, and insisted that he should come to my rooms. Over a glass of wine I warmly thanked him and his brave comrades for saving me. He replied simply that he was more than glad, and that Herr Delbrück had at the first taken steps to make all the searching party pleased; at which ambiguous utterance the maître d'hôtel smiled, while the officer pleaded duty and withdrew.

"But Herr Delbrück," I enquired, "how and why was it that the soldiers searched for me?"

He shrugged his shoulders, as if in depreciation of his own deed, as he replied:

"I was so fortunate as to obtain leave from the commander of the regiment in which I served, to ask for volunteers."

"But how did you know I was lost?" I asked.

"The driver came hither with the remains of his carriage, which had been upset when the horses ran away."

"But surely you would not send a search-party of soldiers merely on this account?"

"On no!" he answered; "but even before the coachman arrived, I had this telegram from the Boyar whose guest you are," and he took from his pocket a telegram which he handed to me, and I read:

BISTRITZ

BE CAREFUL OF MY GUEST—HIS SAFETY IS MOST PRECIOUS TO ME. SHOULD AUGHT HAPPEN TO HIM, OR IF HE BE MISSED, SPARE NOTHING TO FIND HIM AND ENSURE HIS SAFETY. HE IS ENGLISH AND THEREFORE ADVENTUROUS. THERE ARE OFTEN DANGERS FROM SNOW AND WOLVES AND NIGHT. LOSE NOT A MOMENT IF YOU SUSPECT HARM TO HIM. I ANSWER YOUR SEAL WITH MY FORTUNE.—DRACULA

As I held the telegram in my hand, the room seemed to whirl around me; and, if the attentive maître d'hôtel had not caught me, I think I should have fallen. There was something so strange in all this, something so weird and impossible to imagine, that there grew on me a sense of my being in some way the sport of opposite forces—the mere vague idea of which seemed in a way to paralyse me. I was certainly under some form of mysterious protection. From a distant country had come, in the very nick of time, a message that took me out of the danger of the snow-sleep and the jaws of the wolf.

# The Withered Arm

*Thomas Hardy*

## I. A LORN MILKMAID

It was an eighty-cow dairy, and the troop of milkers, regular and super-numerary, were all at work; for, though the time of year was as yet but early April, the feed lay entirely in water-meadows, and the cows were "in full pail". The hour was about six in the evening, and three-fourths of the large, red, rectangular animals having been finished off, there was opportunity for a little conversation.

"He do bring home his bride tomorrow, I hear. They've come as far as Anglebury today."

The voice seemed to proceed from the belly of the cow called Cherry, but the speaker was a milking-woman, whose face was buried in the flank of that motionless beast.

"Hav' anybody seen her?" said another.

There was a negative response from the first. "Though they say she's a rosy-cheeked, tisty-tosty little body enough," she added; and as the milkmaid spoke she turned her face so that she could glance past her cow's tail to the other side of the barton, where a thin, fading woman of thirty milked somewhat apart from the rest.

"Years younger than he, they say," continued the second, with also a glance of reflectiveness in the same direction.

"How old do you call him, then?"

"Thirty or so."

"More like forty," broke in an old milkman near, in a long white pinafore, or "wropper", and with the brim of his hat tied down, so that he looked like a woman. "'A was born before our Great Weir was builded, and I hadn't man's wages when I laved water there."

The discussion waxed so warm that the purr of the milk streams became jerky, till a voice from another cow's belly cried with authority, "Now then, what the Turk do it matter to us about Farmer Lodge's age, or Farmer Lodge's new mis'ess? I shall have to pay him nine pound a year for the rent of every one of the milchers, whatever his age or hers. Get on with your work, or 'twill be dark afore we have done. The evening is pinking in a'ready." This speaker was

the dairyman himself, by whom the milkmaids and men were employed.

Nothing more was said publicly about Farmer Lodge's wedding, but the first woman murmured under her cow to her next neighbour, "'Tis hard for *she*," signifying the thin worn milkmaid aforesaid.

"O no," said the second. "He ha'n't spoke to Rhoda Brook for years."

When the milking was done they washed their pails and hung them on a many-forked stand made as usual of the peeled limb of an oak-tree, set upright in the earth, and resembling a colossal antlered horn. The majority then dispersed in various directions homeward. The thin woman who had not spoken was joined by a boy of twelve or thereabout, and the twain went away up the field also.

Their course lay apart from that of the others, to a lonely spot high above the water-meads, and not far from the border of Egdon Heath, whose dark countenance was visible in the distance as they drew nigh to their home.

"They've just been saying down in barton that your father brings his young wife home from Anglebury tomorrow," the woman observed. "I shall want to send you for a few things to market, and you'll be pretty sure to meet 'em."

"Yes, mother," said the boy. "Is father married then?"

"Yes. . . . You can give her a look, and tell me what she's like, if you do see her."

"Yes, mother."

"If she's dark or fair, and if she's tall—as tall as I. And if she seems like a woman who has ever worked for a living, or one that has been always well off, and has never done anything, and shows marks of the lady on her, as I expect she do."

"Yes."

They crept up the hill in the twilight and entered the cottage. It was built of mud-walls, the surface of which had been washed by many rains into channels and depressions that left none of the original flat face visible; while here and there in the thatch above a rafter showed like a bone protruding through the skin.

She was kneeling down in the chimney-corner, before two pieces of turf laid together with the heather inwards, blowing at the red-hot ashes with her breath till the turves flamed. The radiance lit her pale cheek, and made her dark eyes, that had once been handsome, seem handsome anew. "Yes," she resumed, "see if she is dark or fair, and if you can notice if her hands be white; if not, see if they look as though she had ever done housework or are milker's hands like mine."

The boy again promised, inattentively this time, his mother not observing that he was cutting a notch with his pocket-knife in the beech-backed chair.

## II. THE YOUNG WIFE

The road from Anglebury to Holmstoke is in general level; but there is one place where a sharp ascent breaks its monotony. Farmers homeward-bound from the former market-town, who trot all the rest of the way, walk their horses up this short incline.

The next evening while the sun was yet bright a handsome new gig, with a lemon-coloured body and red wheels, was spinning westward along the level highway at the heels of a powerful mare. The driver was a yeoman in the prime of life, cleanly shaven like an actor, his face being toned to that bluish-vermilion hue which so often graces a thriving farmer's features when returning home after successful dealings in the town. Beside him sat a woman, many years his junior—almost, indeed, a girl. Her face too was fresh in colour, but it was of a totally different quality—soft and evanescent, like the light under a heap of rose-petals.

Few people travelled this way, for it was not a main road; and the long white riband of gravel that stretched before them was empty, save of one small scarce-moving speck, which presently resolved itself into the figure of a boy, who was creeping on at a snail's pace, and continually looking behind him—the heavy bundle he carried being some excuse for, if not the reason of, his dilatoriness. When the bouncing gig-party slowed at the bottom of the incline above mentioned, the pedestrian was only a few yards in front. Supporting the large bundle by putting one hand on his hip, he turned and looked straight at the farmer's wife as though he would read her through and through, pacing along abreast of the horse.

The low sun was full in her face, rendering every feature, shade, and contour distinct, from the curve of her little nostril to the colour of her eyes. The farmer, though he seemed annoyed at the boy's persistent presence, did not order him to get out of the way; and thus the lad preceded them, his hard gaze never leaving her, till they reached the top of the ascent, when the farmer trotted on with relief in his lineaments—having taken no outward notice of the boy whatever.

"How that poor lad stared at me!" said the young wife.

"Yes, dear; I saw that he did."

"He is one of the village, I suppose?"

"One of the neighbourhood. I think he lives with his mother a mile or two off."

"He knows who we are, no doubt?"

"O yes. You must expect to be stared at just at first, my pretty Gertrude."

"I do—though I think the poor boy may have looked at us in the hope we might relieve him of his heavy load, rather than from curiosity."

"O no," said her husband off-handedly. "These country lads will carry a hundredweight once they get it on their backs; besides his pack had more size than weight in it. Now, then, another mile and I shall be able to show you our house in the distance—if it is not too dark before we get there." The wheels spun round, and particles flew from their periphery as before, till a white house of ample dimensions revealed itself, with farm-buildings and ricks at the back.

Meanwhile the boy had quickened his pace, and turning up a by-lane some mile and half short of the white farmstead, ascended towards the leaner pastures, and so on to the cottage of his mother.

She had reached home after her day's milking at the outlying dairy, and was washing cabbage at the doorway in the declining light. "Hold up the net a moment," she said, without preface, as the boy came up.

He flung down his bundle, held the edge of the cabbage-net, and as she filled its meshes with the dripping leaves she went on, "Well, did you see her?"

"Yes; quite plain."

"Is she ladylike?"

"Yes; and more. A lady complete."

"Is she young?"

"Well, she's growed up, and her ways be quite a woman's."

"Of course. What colour is her hair and face?"

"Her hair is lightish, and her face as comely as a live doll's."

"Her eyes, then, are not dark like mine?"

"No—of a bluish turn, and her mouth is very nice and red; and when she smiles, her teeth show white."

"Is she tall?" said the woman sharply.

"I couldn't see. She was sitting down."

"Then do you go to Holmstoke church tomorrow morning: she's sure to be there. Go early and notice her walking in, and come home and tell me if she's taller than I."

"Very well, mother. But why don't you go and see for yourself?"

"*I* go to see her! I wouldn't look up at her if she were to pass my window this instant. She was with Mr Lodge, of course. What did he say or do?"

"Just the same as usual."

"Took no notice of you?"

"None."

Next day the mother put a clean shirt on the boy, and started him off for Holmstoke church. He reached the ancient little pile when the door was just being opened, and he was the first to enter. Taking his seat by the font, he watched all the parishioners file in. The well-to-do Farmer Lodge came nearly last; and his young wife, who accompanied him, walked up the aisle with the shyness natural to a modest woman who had appeared thus for the first time. As all other eyes were fixed upon her, the youth's stare was not noticed now.

When he reached home his mother said, "Well?" before he had entered the room.

"She is not tall. She is rather short," he replied.

"Ah!" said his mother, with satisfaction.

"But she's very pretty—very. In fact, she's lovely." The youthful freshness of the yeoman's wife had evidently made an impression even on the somewhat hard nature of the boy.

"That's all I want to hear," said his mother quickly. "Now, spread the table-cloth. The hare you wired is very tender; but mind that nobody catches you.—You've never told me what sort of hands she had."

"I have never seen 'em. She never took off her gloves."

"What did she wear this morning?"

"A white bonnet and a silver-coloured gown. It whewed and whistled so loud when it rubbed against the pews that the lady coloured up more than ever for very shame at the noise, and pulled it in to keep it from touching; but when she pushed into her seat, it whewed more than ever. Mr Lodge, he seemed pleased, and his waistcoat stuck out, and his great golden seals hung like a lord's; but she seemed to wish her noisy gown anywhere but on her."

"Not she! However, that will do now."

These descriptions of the newly-married couple were continued from time to time by the boy at his mother's request, after any chance encounter he had had with them. But Rhoda Brook, though she might easily have seen young Mrs Lodge for herself by walking a couple of miles, would never attempt an excursion towards the quarter where the farmhouse lay. Neither did she, at the daily milking in the dairyman's yard on Lodge's outlying second farm, ever speak on the subject of the recent marriage. The dairyman, who rented the cows of Lodge, and knew perfectly the tall milkmaid's history, with manly kindliness always kept the gossip in the cow-barton from annoying Rhoda. But the atmosphere thereabout was full of the subject during the first days of Mrs Lodge's arrival; and from her boy's description and the casual words of the other milkers, Rhoda Brook could raise a mental image of the unconscious Mrs Lodge that was realistic as a photograph.

## III. A VISION

One night, two or three weeks after the bridal return, when the boy was gone to bed, Rhoda sat a long time over the turf ashes that she had raked out in front of her to extinguish them. She contemplated so intently the new wife, as presented to her in her mind's eye over the embers, that she forgot the lapse of time. At last, wearied with her day's work, she too retired.

But the figure which had occupied her so much during this and the previous days was not to be banished at night. For the first time Gertrude Lodge visited the supplanted woman in her dreams. Rhoda Brook dreamed—since her assertion that she really saw, before falling asleep, was not to be believed—that the young wife, in the pale silk dress and white bonnet, but with features shockingly distorted, and wrinkled as by age, was sitting upon her chest as she lay. The pressure of Mrs Lodge's person grew heavier; the blue eyes peered cruelly into her face; and then the figure thrust forward its left hand mockingly, so as to make the wedding-ring it wore glitter in Rhoda's eyes. Maddened mentally, and nearly suffocated by pressure, the sleeper struggled; the incubus, still regarding her, withdrew to the foot of the bed, only, however, to come forward by degrees, resume her seat, and flash her left hand as before.

Gasping for breath, Rhoda, in a last desperate effort, swung out her right hand, seized the confronting spectre by its obtrusive left arm, and whirled it backward to the floor, starting up herself as she did so with a low cry.

"O, merciful heaven!" she cried, sitting on the edge of the bed in a cold sweat; "that was not a dream—she was here!"

She could feel her antagonist's arm within her grasp even now—the very flesh and bone of it, as it seemed. She looked on the floor whither she had whirled the spectre, but there was nothing to be seen.

Rhoda Brook slept no more that night, and when she went milking at the next dawn they noticed how pale and haggard she looked. The milk that she drew quivered into the pail; her hand not calmed even yet, and still retained the feel of the arm. She came home to breakfast as wearily as if it had been supper-time.

"What was that noise in your chimmer, mother, last night?" said her son. "You fell off the bed, surely?"

"Did you hear anything fall? At what time?"

"Just when the clock struck two."

She could not explain, and when the meal was done went silently about her household work, the boy assisting her, for he hated going afield on the farms, and she indulged his reluctance. Between eleven and twelve the garden-gate clicked, and she lifted her eyes to the window. At the bottom of the garden, within the gate, stood the woman of her vision. Rhoda seemed transfixed.

"Ah, she said she would come!" exclaimed the boy, also observing her.

"Said so—when? How does she know us?"

"I have seen and spoken to her. I talked to her yesterday."

"I told you," said the mother, flushing indignantly, "never to speak to anybody in that house, or go near the place."

"I did not speak to her till she spoke to me. And I did not go near the place. I met her in the road."

"What did you tell her?"

"Nothing. She said, 'Are you the poor boy who had to bring the heavy load from market?' And she looked at my boots, and said they would not keep my feet dry if it came on wet, because they were so cracked. I told I lived with my mother, and we had enough to do to keep ourselves, and that's how it was; and she said then, 'I'll come and bring you some better boots, and see your mother.' She gives away things to other folks in the meads besides us."

Mrs Lodge was by this time close to the door—not in her silk, as Rhoda had dreamt of in the bed-chamber, but in a morning hat, and gown of common light material, which became her better than silk. On her arm she carried a basket.

The impression remaining from the night's experience was still strong. Brook had almost expected to see the wrinkles, the scorn, and the cruelty on her visitor's face. She would have escaped an interview, had escape been possible. There was, however, no backdoor to the cottage, and in an instant the boy had lifted the latch to Mrs Lodge's gentle knock.

"I see I have come to the right house," said she, glancing at the lad, and smiling. "But I was not sure till you opened the door."

The figure and action were those of the phantom; but her voice was so indescribably sweet, her glance so winning, her smile so tender, so unlike that of Rhoda's midnight visitant, that the latter could hardly believe the evidence of her senses. She was truly glad that she had not hidden away in sheer aversion, as she had been inclined to do. In her basket Mrs Lodge brought the pair of boots that she had promised to the boy, and other useful articles.

At these proofs of a kindly feeling towards her and hers Rhoda's heart reproached her bitterly. This innocent young thing should have her blessing and not her curse. When she left them a light seemed gone from the dwelling. Two days later she came again to know if the boots fitted; and less than a fortnight after that paid Rhoda another call. On this occasion the boy was absent.

"I walk a good deal," said Mrs Lodge, "and your house is the nearest outside our own parish. I hope you are well. You don't look quite well."

Rhoda said she was well enough; and, indeed, though the paler of the two, there was more of the strength that endures in her well-defined features and large frame than in the soft-cheeked young woman before her. The conversation became quite confidential as regarded their powers and weaknesses; and when Mrs Lodge was leaving, Rhoda said, "I hope you will find this air agree with you, ma'am, and not suffer from the damp of the water meads."

The younger one replied that there was not much doubt of it, her general health being usually good. "Though, now you remind me," she added, "I have one little ailment which puzzles me. It is nothing serious, but I cannot make it out."

She uncovered her left hand and arm; and their outline confronted Rhoda's gaze as the exact original of the limb she had beheld and seized in her dream. Upon the pink surface of the arm were faint marks of an unhealthy colour, as if produced by a rough grasp. Rhoda's eyes became riveted on the discolorations; she fancied she discerned in them the shape of her own four fingers.

"How did it happen?" she said mechanically.

"I cannot tell," replied Mrs Lodge, shaking her head. "One night when I was sound asleep, dreaming I was away in some strange place, a pain suddenly shot into my arm there, and was so keen as to awaken me. I must have struck it in the daytime, I suppose, though I don't remember doing so." She added, laughing, "I tell my dear husband that it looks just as if he had flown into a rage and struck me there. O, I daresay it will soon disappear."

"Ha, ha! Yes. . . . On what night did it come?"

Mrs Lodge considered, and said it would be a fortnight ago on the morrow. "When I awoke I could not remember where I was," she added, "till the clock striking two reminded me."

She had named the night and hour of Rhoda's spectral encounter, and Brook felt like a guilty thing. The artless disclosure startled her; she did not reason on the freaks of coincidence; and all the scenery of that ghastly night returned with double vividness to her mind.

"O, can it be," she said to herself, when her visitor had departed, "that I exercise a malignant power over people against my own will?" She knew that she had been slyly called a witch since her fall; but never having understood why that particular stigma had been attached to her, it had passed disregarded. Could this be the explanation, and had such things as this ever happened before?

## IV. A SUGGESTION

The summer drew on, and Rhoda Brook almost dreaded to meet Mrs Lodge again, notwithstanding that her feeling for the young wife amounted well-nigh to affection. Something in her own individuality seemed to convict Rhoda of crime. Yet a fatality sometimes would direct the steps of the latter to the outskirts of Holmstoke whenever she left her house for any other purpose than her daily work; and hence it happened that their next encounter was out of doors. Rhoda could not avoid the subject which had so mystified her, and after the first few words she stammered, "I hope your—arm is well again, ma'am?" She had perceived with consternation that Gertrude Lodge carried her left arm stiffly.

"No; it is not quite well. Indeed it is no better at all; it is rather worse. It pains me dreadfully sometimes."

"Perhaps you had better go to a doctor, ma'am."

She replied that she had already seen a doctor. Her husband had insisted upon her going to one. But the surgeon had not seemed to understand the afflicted limb at all; he had told her to bathe it in hot water, and she had bathed it, but the treatment had done no good.

"Will you let me see it?" said the milkwoman.

Mrs Lodge pushed up her sleeve and disclosed the place, which was a few inches above the wrist. As soon as Rhoda Brook saw it, she could hardly preserve her composure. There was nothing of the nature of a wound, but the arm at that point had a shrivelled look, and the outline of the four fingers appeared more distinct than at the former time. Moreover, she fancied that they were imprinted in precisely the relative position of her clutch upon the arm in the trance; the first finger towards Gertrude's wrist, and the fourth towards her elbow.

What the impress resembled seemed to have struck Gertrude herself since their last meeting. "It looks almost like finger-marks," she said; adding with a faint laugh, "my husband says it is as if some witch, or the devil himself, had taken hold of me there, and blasted the flesh."

Rhoda shivered. "That's fancy," she said hurriedly. "I wouldn't mind it, if I were you."

"I shouldn't so much mind it," said the younger, with hesitation, "if—if I hadn't a notion that it makes my husband—dislike me—no, love me less. Men think so much of personal appearance."

"Some do—he for one."

"Yes; and he was very proud of mine, at first."

"Keep your arm covered from his sight."

"Ah—he knows the disfigurement is there!" She tried to hide the tears that filled her eyes.

"Well, ma'am, I earnestly hope it will go away soon."

And so the milkwoman's mind was chained anew to the subject by a horrid sort of spell as she returned home. The sense of having been guilty of an act of malignity increased, affect as she might to ridicule her superstition. In her secret heart Rhoda did not altogether object to a slight diminution of her successor's beauty, by whatever means it had come about; but she did not wish to inflict upon her physical pain. For though this pretty young woman had rendered impossible any reparation which Lodge might have made Rhoda for his past conduct, everything like resentment at the unconscious usurpation had quite passed away from the elder's mind.

If the sweet and kindly Gertrude Lodge only knew of the dream-scene in the bed-chamber, what would she think? Not to inform her of it seemed treachery in the presence of her friendliness; but tell she could not of her own accord—neither could she devise a remedy.

She mused upon the matter the greater part of the night; and the next day, after the morning milking, set out to obtain another glimpse of Gertrude Lodge if she could, being held to her by a gruesome fascination. By watching the house from a distance the milkmaid was presently able to discern the farmer's wife in a ride she was taking alone—probably to join her husband in some distant field. Mrs Lodge perceived her, and cantered in her direction.

"Good morning, Rhoda!" Gertrude said, when she had come up. "I was going to call."

Rhoda noticed that Mrs Lodge held the reins with some difficulty.

"I hope—the bad arm," said Rhoda.

"They tell me there is possibly one way by which I might be able to find out the cause, and so perhaps the cure, of it," replied the other anxiously. "It is by going to some clever man over in Egdon Heath. They did not know if he was still alive—and I cannot remember his name at the moment; but they said that you knew more of his movements than anybody else hereabout, and could tell me if he were still to be consulted. Dear me—what was his name? But you know."

"Not Conjuror Trendle?" said her thin companion, turning pale.

"Trendle—yes. Is he alive?"

"I believe so," said Rhoda, with reluctance.

"Why do you call him conjuror?"

"Well—they say—they used to say he was a—he had powers other folks have not."

"O, how could my people be so superstitious at to recommend a man of that sort! I thought they meant some medical man. I shall think no more of him."

Rhoda looked relieved, and Mrs Lodge rode on. The milkwoman had inwardly seen, from the moment she heard of her having been mentioned as a reference for this man, that there must exist a sarcastic feeling among the work-folk that a sorceress would know the whereabouts of the exorcist. They suspected her, then. A short time ago this would have given no concern to a women of her common-sense. But she had a haunting reason to be superstitious now; and she had been seized with sudden dread that this Conjuror Trendle might name her as the malignant influence which was blasting the fair person of Gertrude, and so lead her friend to hate her for ever, and to treat her as some fiend in human shape.

But all was not over. Two days after, a shadow intruded into the window-pattern thrown on Rhoda Brook's floor by the afternoon sun. The woman opened the door at once, almost breathlessly.

"Are you alone?" said Gertrude. She seemed to be no less harassed and anxious than Brook herself.

"Yes," said Rhoda.

"The place on my arm seems worse, and troubles me!" the young farmer's wife went on. "It is so mysterious! I do hope it will not be an incurable wound. I have again been thinking of what they said about Conjuror Trendle. I don't really believe in such men, but I should not mind just visiting him, from curiosity—though on no account must my husband know. It is far to where he lives?"

"Yes—five miles," said Rhoda backwardly. "In the heart of Egdon."

"Well, I should have to walk. Could not you go with me to show me the way—say to-morrow afternoon?"

"O, not I; that is——," the milkwoman murmured, with a start of dismay. Again the dread seized her that something to do with her fierce act in the dream might be revealed, and her character in the eyes of the most useful friend she had ever had be ruined irretrievably.

Mrs Lodge urged, and Rhoda finally assented, though with much misgiving. Sad as the journey would be to her, she could not conscientiously stand in the way of a possible remedy for her patron's strange affliction. It was agreed that, to escape suspicion of their mystic intent, they should meet at the edge of the heath at the corner of a plantation which was visible from the spot where they now stood.

## V. CONJUROR TRENDLE

By the next afternoon Rhoda would have done anything to escape this inquiry. But she had promised to go. Moreover, there was a horrid fascination at times in becoming instrumental in throwing such possible light on her own character as would reveal her to be something greater in the occult world than she had ever herself suspected.

She started just before the time of day mentioned between them, and half-an-hour's brisk walking brought her to the south-eastern extension of the Egdon tract of country, where the fir plantation was. A slight figure, cloaked and veiled, was already there. Rhoda recognized, almost with a shudder, that Mrs Lodge bore her left arm in a sling.

They hardly spoke to each other, and immediately set out on their climb into the interior of this solemn country, which stood high above the rich alluvial soil they had left half-an-hour before. It was a long walk; thick clouds made the atmosphere dark, though it was as yet only early afternoon; and the wind howled dismally over the slopes of the heath—not improbably the same heath which had witnessed the agony of the Wessex King Ina, presented to after-ages as Lear. Gertrude Lodge talked most, Rhoda replying with monosyllabic preoccupation. She had a strange dislike to walking on the side of her companion where hung the afflicted arm, moving round to the other when inadvertently near it. Much heather had been brushed by their feet when they descended upon a cart-track, beside which stood the house of the man they sought.

He did not profess his remedial practices openly, or care anything about their continuance, his direct interest being those of a dealer in furze, turf, "sharp sand", and other local products. Indeed, he affected not to believe largely in his own powers, and when warts that had been shown him for cure miraculously disappeared—which it must be owned they infallibly did—he would say lightly, "O, I only drink a glass of grog upon 'em at your expense—perhaps it's all chance," and immediately turn the subject.

He was at home when they arrived, having in fact seen them descending into his valley. He was a grey-bearded man, with a reddish face, and he looked singularly at Rhoda the first moment he beheld her. Mrs Lodge told him her errand; and then with words of self-disparagement he examined her arm.

"Medicine can't cure it," he said promptly. "'Tis the work of an enemy."

Rhoda shrank into herself, and drew back.

"An enemy? What enemy?" asked Mrs Lodge.

He shook his head. "That's best known to yourself," he said. "If you like, I can show the person to you, though I shall not myself know who it is. I can do no more; and don't wish to do that."

She pressed him; on which he told Rhoda to wait outside where she stood, and took Mrs Lodge into the room. It opened immediately from the door; and, as the latter remained ajar, Rhoda Brook could see the proceedings without taking part in them. He brought a tumbler from the dresser, nearly filled it with water, and fetching an egg, prepared it in some private way; after which he broke it on the edge of the glass, so that the white went in and the yolk remained. As it was getting gloomy, he took the glass and its contents to the window, and told Gertrude to watch the mixture closely. They leant over the table together, and the milkwoman could see the opaline hue of the egg-fluid changing form as it sank in the water, but she was not near enough to define the shape that it assumed.

"Do you catch the likeness of any face or figure as you look?" demanded the conjuror of the young woman.

She murmured a reply, in tones so low as to be inaudible to Rhoda, and continued to gaze intently into the glass. Rhoda turned, and walked a few steps away.

When Mrs Lodge came out, and her face was met by the light, it appeared exceedingly pale—as pale as Rhoda's—against the sad dun shades of the upland's garniture. Trendle shut the door behind her, and they at once started homeward together. But Rhoda perceived that her companion had quite changed.

"Did he charge much?" she asked tentatively.

"O no—nothing. He would not take a farthing," said Gertrude.

"And what did you see?" inquired Rhoda.

"Nothing I—care to speak of." The constraint in her manner was remarkable; her face was so rigid as to wear an oldened aspect, faintly suggestive of the face in Rhoda's bed-chamber.

"Was it you who first proposed coming here?" Mrs Lodge suddenly inquired, after a long pause. "How very odd, if you did!"

"No. But I am not sorry we have come, all things considered," she replied. For the first time a sense of triumph possessed her, and she did not altogether deplore that the young thing at her side should learn that their lives had been antagonized by other influences than their own.

The subject was no more alluded to during the long and dreary walk home. But in some way or other a story was whispered about the many-dairied lowland that winter that Mrs Lodge's gradual loss of the use of her left arm was owing to her being "overlooked" by Rhoda Brook. The latter kept her own counsel about the incubus, but her face grew sadder and thinner; and in the spring she and her boy disappeared from the neighbourhood of Holmstoke.

## VI. A SECOND ATTEMPT

Half a dozen years passed away, and Mr and Mrs Lodge's married experience sank into prosiness, and worse. The farmer was usually gloomy and silent: the woman whom he had wooed for her grace and beauty was contorted and disfigured in the left limb; moreover, she had brought him no child, which rendered it likely that he would be the last of a family who had occupied that valley for some two hundred years. He thought of Rhoda Brook and her son; and feared this might be a judgment from heaven upon him.

The once blithe-hearted and enlightened Gertrude was changing into an irritable, superstitious woman, whose whole time was given to experimenting upon her ailment with every quack remedy she came across. She was honestly attached to her husband, and was ever secretly hoping against hope to win back his heart again by regaining some at least of her personal beauty. Hence it arose that her closet was lined with bottles, packets, and ointment-pots of every description—nay, bunches of mystic herbs, charms, and books of necromancy, which in her schoolgirl time she would have ridiculed as folly.

"Damned if you won't poison yourself with these apothecary messes and witch mixtures some time or other," said her husband, when his eye chanced to fall upon the multitudinous array.

She did not reply, but turned her sad, soft glance upon him in such heart-swollen reproach that he looked sorry for his words, and added, "I only meant it for your good, you know, Gertrude."

"I'll clear out the whole lot, and destroy them," said she huskily, "and try such remedies no more!"

"You want somebody to cheer you," he observed. "I once thought of adopting a boy; but he is too old now. And he is gone away I don't know where."

She guessed to whom he alluded; for Rhoda Brook's story had in the course of years become known to her; though not a word had ever passed between her husband and herself on the subject. Neither had she ever spoken to him of her visit to Conjuror Trendle, and of what was revealed to her, or she thought was revealed to her, by that solitary heathman.

She was now five-and-twenty; but she seemed older. "Six years of marriage, and only a few months of love," she sometimes whispered to herself. And then she thought of the apparent cause, and said, with a tragic glance at her withering limb, "If I could only again be as I was when he first saw me!"

She obediently destroyed her nostrums and charms; but there remained a hankering wish to try something else—some other sort of cure altogether. She had never revisited Trendle since she had been conducted to the house of the solitary by Rhoda against her will; but it now suddenly occurred to Gertrude that she would, in a last desperate effort at deliverance from this seeming curse, again seek out the man, if he yet lived. He was entitled to a certain credence, for the indistinct form he had raised in the glass had undoubtedly resembled the only woman in the world who—as she now knew, though not then—could have a reason for bearing her ill-will. The visit should be paid.

This time she went alone, though she nearly got lost on the heath, and roamed a considerable distance out of her way. Trendle's house was reached at last, however: he was not indoors, and instead of waiting at the cottage, she went to where his bent figure was pointed out to her at work a long way off. Trendle remembered her, and laying down the handful of furze-roots which he was gathering and throwing into a heap, he offered to accompany her in her homeward direction, as the distance was considerable and the days were short. So they walked together, his head bowed nearly to the earth, and his form of a colour with it.

"You can send away warts and other excrescences, I know," she said; "why can't you send away this?" And the arm was uncovered.

"You think too much of my powers!" said Trendle; "and I am old and weak now, too. No, no; it is too much for me to attempt in my own person. What have ye tried?"

She named to him some of the hundred medicaments and counter-spells which she had adopted from time to time. He shook his head.

"Some were good enough," he said approvingly; "but not many of them for such as this. This is of the nature of a blight, not of the nature of a wound; and if you ever do throw it off, it will be all at once."

"If I only could!"

"There is only one chance of doing it known to me. It has never failed in kindred afflictions—that I can declare. But it is hard to carry out, and especially for a woman."

"Tell me!" said she.

"You must touch with the limb the neck of a man who's been hanged."

She started a little at the image he had raised.

"Before he's cold—just after he's cut down," continued the conjuror impassively.

"How can that do good?"

"It will turn the blood and change the constitution. But, as I say, to do it is hard. You must go to the jail when there's a hanging, and wait for him when he's brought off the gallows. Lots have done it, though perhaps not such pretty women as you. I used to send dozens for skin complaints. But that was in former times. The last I sent was in '13—near twelve years ago."

He had no more to tell her; and when he had put her into a straight track homeward, turned and left her, refusing all money as at first.

## VII. A RIDE

The communication sank deep into Gertrude's mind. Her nature was rather a timid one; and probably of all remedies that the white wizard could have suggested there was not one which would have filled her with so much aversion as this, not to speak of the immense obstacles in the way of its adoption.

Casterbridge, the county-town, was a dozen or fifteen miles off; and though in those days, when men were executed for horse-stealing, arson, and burglary, an assize seldom passed without a hanging, it was not likely that she could get access to the body of the criminal unaided. And the fear of her husband's anger made her reluctant to breathe a word of Trendle's suggestion to him or to anybody about him.

She did nothing for months, and patiently bore her disfigurement as before. But her women's nature, craving for renewed love, through the medium of renewed beauty (she was but twenty-five), was ever stimulating her to try what, at any rate, could hardly do her any harm. "What came by a spell will go by a spell surely," she would say. Whenever her imagination pictured the act she shrank in terror from the possibility of it: then the words of the conjuror, "It will turn your blood," were seen to be capable of a scientific no less than a ghastly interpretation; the mastering desire returned, and urged her on again.

There was at this time but one county paper, and that her husband only occasionally borrowed. But old-fashioned days had old-fashioned means, and news was extensively conveyed by word of mouth from market to market, or from fair to fair, so that, whenever such an event as an execution was about to take place, few within a radius of twenty miles were ignorant of the coming sight; and, so far as Holmstoke was concerned, some enthusiasts had been known to walk all the way to Casterbridge and back in one day, solely to witness the spectacle. The next assizes were in March; and when Gertrude Lodge heard that they had been held, she inquired stealthily at the inn as to the result, as soon as she could find opportunity.

She was, however, too late. The time at which the sentences were to be carried out had arrived, and to make the journey and obtain admission at such short notice required at least her husband's assistance. She dared not tell him, for she had found by delicate experiment that these smouldering village beliefs made him furious if mentioned, partly because he half entertained them himself. It was therefore necessary to wait for another opportunity.

Her determination received a fillip from learning that two epileptic children had attended from this very village of Holmstoke many years before with beneficial results, though the experiment had been strongly condemned by the neighbouring clergy. April, May, June, passed; and it is no overstatement to say that by the end of the last-named month Gertrude well-nigh longed for the death of a fellow-creature. Instead of her formal prayers each night, her unconscious prayer was, "O Lord, hang some guilty or innocent person soon!"

This time she made earlier inquiries, and was altogether more systematic in her proceedings. Moreover, the season was summer, between the haymaking and the harvest, and in the leisure thus afforded him her husband had been holiday-taking away from home.

The assizes were in July, and she went to the inn as before. There was to be one execution—only one—for arson.

Her greatest problem was not how to get to Casterbridge, but what means she should adopt for obtaining admission to the jail. Though access for such purposes had formerly never been denied, the custom had fallen into desuetude; and in contemplating her possible difficulties, she was again almost driven to fall back upon her husband. But, on sounding him about the assizes, he was so uncommunicative, so more than usually cold, that she did not proceed, and decided that whatever she did she would do alone.

Fortune, obdurate hitherto, showed her unexpected favour. On the Thursday before the Saturday fixed for the execution, Lodge remarked to her that he was going away from home for another day or two on business at a fair, and that he was sorry he could not take her with him.

She exhibited on this occasion so much readiness to stay at home that he looked at her in surprise. Time had been when she would have shown deep disappointment at the loss of such a jaunt. However, he lapsed into his usual taciturnity, and on the day named left Holmstoke.

It was now her turn. She at first had thought of driving, but on reflection held that driving would not do, since it would necessitate her keeping to the turnpike road, and so increase by tenfold the risk of her ghastly errand being found out. She decided to ride, and avoid the beaten track, notwithstanding that in her husband's stables there was no animal just at present which by any stretch of imagination could be considered a lady's mount, in spite of his promise before marriage to always keep a mare for her. He had, however, many cart-horses, fine ones of their kind; and among the rest was a serviceable creature, an equine Amazon, with a back as broad as a sofa, on which Gertrude had occasionally taken an airing when unwell. This horse she chose.

On Friday afternoon one of the men brought it round. She was dressed, and before going down looked at her shrivelled arm. "Ah!" she said to it, "if it had not been for you this terrible ordeal would have been saved me!"

When strapping up the bundle in which she carried a few articles of clothing, she took occasion to say to the servant, "I take these in case I should not get back tonight from the person I am going to visit. Don't be alarmed if I am not in by ten, and close up the house as usual. I shall be at home tomorrow for certain." She meant then to tell her husband privately: the deed accomplished was not like the deed projected. He would almost certainly forgive her.

And then the pretty, palpitating Gertrude Lodge went from her husband's homestead; but though her goal was Casterbridge she did not take the direct route thither through Stickleford. Her cunning course at first was in precisely the opposite direction. As soon as she was out of sight, however, she turned to the left, by a road which led into Egdon, and on entering the heath wheeled round, and set out in the true course, due westerly. A more private way down the county could not be imagined; and as to direction, she had merely to keep her horse's head to a point a little to the right of the sun. She knew that she would light upon a furze-cutter or cottager of some sort from time to time, from whom she might correct her bearing.

Though the date was comparatively recent, Egdon was much less fragmentary in character than now. The attempts—successful and otherwise—at cultivation on the lower slopes, which intrude and break up the original heath into small detached heaths, had not been carried far; Enclosure Acts had not taken effect, and the banks and fences which now exclude the cattle of those villagers who formerly enjoyed rights of commonage thereon, and the carts of those who had turbary privileges which kept them in firing all the year round, were not erected. Gertrude, therefore, rode along with no other obstacles than the prickly furze-bushes, the mats of heather, the white water-courses, and the natural steeps and declivities of the ground.

Her horse was sure, if heavy-footed and slow, and though a draught animal, was easy-paced; had it been otherwise, she was not a woman who could have ventured to ride over such a bit of country with a half-dead arm. It was therefore nearly eight o'clock when she drew rein to breathe her bearer on the last outlying high point of heath-land towards Casterbridge, previous to leaving Egdon for the cultivated valleys.

She halted before a pool called Rushy-pond, flanked by the ends of two hedges; a railing ran through the centre of the pond, dividing it in half. Over the railing she saw the low green country; over the green trees the roofs of the town; over the roofs a white flat façade, denoting the entrance to the county jail. On the roof of this front specks were moving about; they seemed to be workmen erecting something. Her flesh crept. She descended slowly, and was soon amid corn-fields and pastures. In another half-hour, when it was almost dusk, Gertrude reached the White Hart, the first inn of the town on that side.

Little surprise was excited by her arrival; farmer's wives rode on horseback then more than they do now; though, for that matter, Mrs Lodge was not imagined to be a wife at all; the innkeeper supposed her some harum-skarum young woman who had come to attend "hang-fair" next day. Neither her husband nor herself ever dealt in Casterbridge market, so that she was unknown. While dismounting she beheld a crowd of boys standing at the door of a harness-maker's shop just above the inn, looking inside it with deep interest.

"What's going on there?" she asked of the ostler.

"Making the rope for tomorrow."

She throbbed responsively, and contracted her arm.

"'Tis sold by the inch afterwards," the man continued. "I could get you a bit, miss, for nothing, if you'd like?"

She hastily repudiated any such wish, all the more from a curious creeping feeling that the condemned wretch's destiny was becoming interwoven with her own; and having engaged a room for the night, sat down to think.

Up to this time she had formed but the vaguest notions about her means of obtaining access to the prison. The words of the cunning-man returned to her mind. He had implied that she should use her beauty, impaired though it was, as a pass-key. In her inexperience she knew little about jail functionaries; she had heard of a high-sheriff and an under-sheriff, but dimly only. She knew, however, that there must be a hangman, and to the hangman she determined to apply.

## VIII. A WATER-SIDE HERMIT

At this date, and for several years after, there was a hangman to almost every jail. Gertrude found, on inquiry, that the Casterbridge official dwelt in a lonely cottage by a deep slow river flowing under the cliff on which the prison buildings were situate—the stream being the self-same one, though she did not know it, which watered the Stickleford and Holmstoke meads lower down in its course.

Having changed her dress, and before she had eaten or drunk—for she could not take her ease till she had ascertained some particulars—Gertrude pursued her way by a path along the water-side to the cottage indicated. Passing thus the outskirts of the jail, she discerned on the level roof over the gateway three rectangular lines against the sky, where the specks had been moving in her distant view; she recognized what the erection was, and passed quickly on. Another hundred yards brought her to the executioner's house, which a boy pointed out. It stood close to the same stream, and was hard by a weir, the waters of which emitted a steady roar.

While she stood hesitating the door opened, and an old man came forth shading a candle with one hand. Locking the door on the outside, he turned to a flight of wooden steps fixed against the end of the cottage, and began to ascend them, this being evidently the staircase to his bedroom. Gertrude hastened forward, but by the time she reached the foot of the ladder he was at the top. She called to him loudly enough to be heard above the roar of the weir; he looked down and said, "What d'ye want here?"

"To speak to you a minute."

The candle-light, such as it was, fell upon her imploring, pale, up-turned face, and Davies (as the hangman was called) backed down the ladder. "I was just going to bed," he said; "'Early to bed and early to rise,' but I don't mind stopping a minute for such a one as you. Come into the house." He reopened the door, and preceded her to the room within.

The implements of his daily work, which was that of a jobbing gardener, stood in a corner, and seeing probably that she looked rural, he said, "If you want me to undertake country work I can't come, for I never leave Casterbridge for gentle nor simple—not I. My real calling is officer of justice," he added formally.

"Yes, yes! That's it. Tomorrow!"

"Ah! I thought so. Well, what's the matter about that? 'Tis no use to come here about the knot—folks do come continually, but I tell 'em one knot is as merciful as another if ye keep it under the ear. Is the unfortunate man a relation; or, I should say, perhaps" (looking at her dress) "a person who's been in your employ?"

"No. What time is the execution?"

"The same as usual—twelve o' clock, or as soon after the London mail-coach gets in. We always wait for that, in case of a reprieve."

"O—a reprieve—I hope not!" she said involuntarily.

"Well—hee, hee!—as a matter of business, so do I! But still if ever a young fellow deserved to be let off, this one does; only just turned eighteen, and only present by chance when the rick was fired. Howsomever, there's not much risk of it, as they are obliged to make an example of him, there having been so much destruction of property that way lately."

"I mean," she explained, "that I want to touch him for a charm, a cure of an affliction, by the advice of a man who has proved the virtue of the remedy."

"O yes, miss! Now I understand. I've had such people come in past years. But it didn't strike me that you looked a sort to require blood-turning. What's the complaint? The wrong kind for this, I'll be bound."

"My arm." She reluctantly showed the withered skin.

"Ah!—'tis all a-scram!" said the hangman, examining it.

"Yes," said she.

"Well," he continued, with interest, "that *is* the class o' subject, I'm bound to admit! I like the look of the wownd; it is truly as suitable for the cure as any I ever saw. 'Twas a knowing-man that sent 'ee, whoever he was."

"You can contrive for me all that's necessary?" she said breathlessly.

"You should really have gone to the governor of the jail, and your doctor with 'ee, and given your name and address—that's how it used to be done, if I recollect. Still, perhaps, I can manage it for a trifling fee."

"O, thank you! I would rather do it this way, as I should like it kept private."

"Lover not to know, eh?"

"No—husband."

"Aha! Very well. I'll get 'ee a touch of the corpse."

"Where is it now?" she said, shuddering.

"It?—*he*, you mean; he's living yet. Just inside that little small winder up there in the glum." He signified the jail on the cliff above.

She thought of her husband and her friends. "Yes, of course," she said; "and how am I to proceed?"

He took her to the door. "Now, do you be waiting at the little wicket in the wall, that you'll find up there in the lane, not later than one o'clock. I will open it from the inside, as I shan't come home to dinner till he's cut down. Good-night. Be punctual; and if you don't want anybody to know 'ee, wear a veil. Ah—once I had such a daughter as you!"

She went away, and climbed the path above, to assure herself that she would be able to find the wicket next day. Its outline was soon visible to her—a narrow opening in the outer wall of the prison precincts. The steep was so great that, having reached the wicket, she stopped a moment to breathe; and, looking back upon the water-side cot, saw the hangman once again ascending his outdoor staircase. He entered the loft or chamber to which it led, and in a few minutes extinguished his light.

The town clock struck ten, and she returned to the White Hart as she had come.

## IX. A RENCOUNTER

It was one o'clock on Saturday. Gertrude Lodge, having been admitted to the jail as above described, was sitting in a waiting-room within the second gate, which stood under a classic archway of ashlar, then comparatively modern, and bearing the inscription, "COVNTY JAIL: 1793". This had been the façade she saw from the heath the day before. Near at hand was a passage to the roof on which the gallows stood.

The town was thronged, and the market suspended; but Gertrude had seen scarcely a soul. Having kept her room till the hour of the appointment, she had proceeded to the spot by a way which avoided the open space below the cliff where the spectators had gathered; but she could, even now, hear the multitudinous babble of their voices, out of which rose at intervals the hoarse creak of a single voice uttering the words, "Last dying speech and confession!" There had been no reprieve, and the execution was over; but the crowd still waited to see the body taken down.

Soon the persistent woman heard a trampling overhead, then a hand beckoned to her, and, following directions, she went out and crossed the inner paved court beyond the gatehouse, her knees trembling so that she could scarcely walk. One of her arms was out of its sleeve, and only covered by her shawl.

On the spot at which she had now arrived there were two trestles, and before she could think of their purpose she heard heavy feet descending stairs somewhere at her back. Turn her head she would not, or could not, and, rigid in this position, she was conscious of a rough coffin passing her shoulder, borne by four men. It was open, and in it lay the body of a young man, wearing the smockfrock of a rustic, and fustian breeches. The corpse had been thrown into the coffin so hastily that the skirt of the smockfrock was hanging over. The burden was temporarily deposited on the trestles.

By this time the young woman's state was such that a grey mist seemed to float before her eyes, on account of which, and the veil she wore, she could scarcely discern anything: it was as though she had nearly died, but was held up by a sort of galvanism.

"Now!" said a voice close at hand, and she was just conscious that the word had been addressed to her.

By a last strenuous effort she advanced, at the same time hearing persons approaching behind her. She bared her poor curst arm; and Davies, uncovering the face of the corpse, took Gertrude's hand, and held it so that her arm lay across the dead man's neck, upon a line the colour of an unripe blackberry, which surrounded it.

Gertrude shrieked: "the turn o' the blood," predicted by the conjuror, had taken place. But at that moment a second shriek rent the air of the enclosure: it was not Gertrude's, and its effect upon her was to make her start round.

Immediately behind her stood Rhoda Brook, her face drawn, and her eyes red with weeping. Behind Rhoda stood Gertrude's own husband; his countenance lined, his eyes dim, but without a tear,

"D—n you! what are you doing here?" he said hoarsely.

"Hussy—to come between us and our child now!" cried Rhoda. "This is the meaning of what Satan showed me in the vision! You are like her at last!" And clutching the bare arm of the younger woman, she pulled her unresistingly back against the wall. Immediately Brook had loosened her hold the fragile young Gertrude slid down against the feet of her husband. When he lifted her up she was unconscious.

The mere sight of the twain had been enough to suggest to her that the dead young man was Rhoda's son. At that time the relatives of an executed convict had the privilege of claiming the body for burial, if they chose to do so; and it was for this purpose that Lodge was awaiting the inquest with Rhoda. He had been summoned by her as soon as the young man was taken in the crime, and at different times since; and he had attended in court during the trial. This was the "holiday" he had been indulging in of late. The two wretched parents had wished to avoid exposure; and hence had come themselves for the body, a waggon and sheet for its conveyance and covering being in waiting outside.

Gertrude's case was so serious that it was deemed advisable to call to her the surgeon who was at hand. She was taken out of the jail into the town; but she never reached home alive. Her delicate vitality, sapped perhaps by the paralyzed arm, collapsed under the double shock that followed the severe strain, physical and mental, to which she had subjected herself during the previous twenty-four hours. Her blood had been "turned" indeed—too far. Her death took place in the town three days after.

Her husband was never seen in Casterbridge again; once only in the old market-place at Anglebury, which he had so much frequented, and very seldom in public anywhere. Burdened at first with moodiness and remorse, he eventually changed for the better, and appeared as a chastened and thoughtful man. Soon after attending the funeral of his poor young wife he took steps towards giving up the farms in Holmstoke and the adjoining parish, and, having sold every head of his stock, he went away to Port-Bredy, at the other end of the county, living there in solitary lodgings till his death two years later of a painless decline. It was then found that he had bequeathed the whole of his not inconsiderable property to a reformatory for boys, subject to the payment of a small annuity to Rhoda Brook, if she could be found to claim it.

For some time she could not be found; but eventually she reappeared in her old parish—absolutely refusing, however, to have anything to do with the provision made for her. Her monotonous milking at the dairy was resumed, and followed for many long years, till her form became bent, and her once abundant dark hair white and worn away at the forehead—perhaps by long pressure against the cows. Here, sometimes, those who knew her experiences would stand and observe her, and wonder what sombre thoughts were beating inside that impassive, wrinkled brow, to the rhythm of the alternating milk-streams.

*Blackwood's Magazine*,
January 1888.

# The Ghostly Rental

*Henry James*

I was in my twenty-second year, and I had just left college. I was at liberty to choose my career, and I chose it with much promptness. I afterwards renounced it, in truth, with equal ardour, but I have never regretted those two youthful years of perplexed and excited, but also of agreeable and fruitful experiment. I had a taste for theology, and during my college term I had been an admiring reader of Dr Channing. This was theology of a grateful and succulent savour; it seemed to offer one the rose of faith delightfully stripped of its thorns. And then (for I rather think this had something to do with it), I had taken a fancy to the Old Divinity School. I have always had an eye to the back scene in the human drama, and it seemed to me that I might play my part with a fair chance of applause (from myself at least), in that detached and tranquil home of mild casuistry, with its respectable avenue on one side, and its prospect of green fields and contact with acres of woodland on the other. Cambridge, for the lovers of woods and fields, has changed for the worse since those days, and the precinct in question has forfeited much of its mingled pastoral and scholastic quietude. It was then a college-hall in the woods—a charming mixture. What it is now has nothing to do with my story; and I have no doubt that there are still doctrine-haunted young seniors who, as they stroll near it in the summer dusk, promise themselves, later, to taste of its fine leisurely quality. For myself, I was not disappointed. I established myself in a great square, low-browed room, with deep window-benches; I hung prints from Overbeck and Ary Scheffer on the walls; I arranged my books, with great refinement of classification, in the alcoves beside the high chimney-shelf, and I began to read Plotinus and St Augustine. Among my companions were two or three men of ability and of good fellowship, with whom I occasionally brewed a fireside bowl; and with adventurous reading, deep discourse, potations conscientiously shallow, and long country walks, my initiation into the clerical mystery progressed agreeably enough.

With one of my comrades I formed an especial friendship, and we passed a great deal of time together. Unfortunately he had a chronic weakness of one of his knees, which compelled him to lead a very sedentary life, and as I was a methodical pedestrian, this made some difference in our habits. I used often to stretch away for my daily ramble, with no companion but the stick in my hand or the book in my pocket. But in the use of my legs and the sense of unstinted open air, I have always found company enough. I should, perhaps, add that in the enjoyment of a very sharp pair of eyes, I found something of a social pleasure. My eyes and I were on excellent terms; they were indefatigable observers of all wayside incidents, and so long as they were amused I was contented. It is, indeed, owing to their inquisitive habits that I came into possession of this remarkable story. Much of the country about the old College town is pretty now, but it was prettier thirty years ago. That multitudinous eruption of domiciliary paste-board which now graces the landscape, in the direction of the low, blue Waltham Hills, had not yet taken place; there were no genteel cottages to put the shabby meadows and scrubby orchards to shame—a juxtaposition by which, in later years, neither element of the contrast has gained. Certain crooked crossroads, then, as I remember them, were more deeply and naturally rural, and the solitary dwellings on the long grassy slopes beside them, under the tall, customary elm that curved its foliage in mid-air like the outward dropping ears of a girdled wheatsheaf, sat with their shingled hoods well pulled down on their ears, and no prescience whatever of the fashion of French roofs—weather-wrinkled old peasant women, as you might call them, quietly wearing the native coif, and never dreaming of mounting bonnets, and indecently exposing their venerable brows. That winter was what is called an "open" one; there was much cold, but little snow; the roads were firm and free, and I was rarely compelled by the weather to forgo my exercise. One grey December afternoon I had sought it in the direction of the adjacent town of Medford, and I was retracing my steps at an even pace, and watching the pale, cold tints—the transparent amber and faded rose-colour—which curtained, in wintry fashion, the western sky, and reminded me of a sceptical smile on the lips of a beautiful woman. I came, as dusk was falling, to a narrow road which I had never traversed and which I imagined offered me a short cut homeward. I was about three miles away; I was late, and would have been thankful to make them two. I diverged, walked some ten minutes, and then perceived that the road had a very unfrequented air. The wheel-ruts looked old; the stillness seemed peculiarly sensible. And yet down the road stood a house, to that it must in some degree have been a thoroughfare. On one side was a high, natural embankment, on the top of which was perched an apple-orchard, whose tangled boughs made a stretch of coarse black lace-work, hung across the coldly rosy west. In a short time I came to the house, and I immediately found myself interested in it. I stopped in front of it gazing hard, I hardly knew why, but with a vague mixture of curiosity and timidity. It was a house like most of the houses thereabouts, except that it was decidedly a handsome specimen of its class. It stood on a grassy slope, it had its tall, impartially drooping elm beside it, and its old black well-cover at its shoulder. But it was of very large proportions, and it had a striking look of solidity and stoutness of timber. It had lived to a good old age, too, for the woodwork on its doorway and under its eaves, carefully and abundantly carved, referred it to the middle, at the latest, of the last century. All this had once been painted white, but the broad back of time, leaning against the door-posts for a hundred years, had laid bare the grain of the wood. Behind the house stretched an orchard of apple-trees, more gnarled and fantastic than usual, and wearing, in the deepening dusk, a blighted and exhausted aspect. All the windows of the house had rusty shutters, without slats, and these were closely drawn. There was no sign of life about it; it looked blank, bare and vacant, and yet, as I lingered near it, it seemed to have a familiar meaning—an audible eloquence. I have always thought of the impression made upon me at first sight, by that grey colonial dwelling, as a proof that induction may sometimes be near akin to divination; for after all, there was nothing on the face of the matter to warrant the very serious induction that I made. I fell back and crossed the road. The last red light of the sunset disengaged itself, as it was about to vanish, and rested faintly for a moment on the time-silvered front of the old house. It touched, with perfect regularity, the series of small panes in the fan-shaped window above the door, and twinkled there fantastically. Then it died away, and left the place more intensely sombre. At this moment, I said to myself with the accent of profound conviction—"The house is simply haunted!"

Somehow, immediately, I believed it, and so long as I was not shut up inside, the idea gave me pleasure. It was implied in the aspect of the house, and it explained it. Half an hour before, if I had been asked, I would have said, as befitted a young man who was explicitly cultivating cheerful views of the supernatural, that there were no such things as haunted houses. But the dwelling before me gave a vivid meaning to the empty words; it had been spiritually blighted.

The longer I looked at it, the intenser seemed the secret that it held. I walked all round it, I tried to peep here and there, through a crevice in the shutters, and I took a puerile satisfaction in laying my hand on the door-knob and gently turning it. If the door had yielded, would I have gone in?—would I have penetrated the dusky stillness? My audacity, fortunately, was not put to the test. The portal was admirably solid, and I was unable even to shake it. At last I turned away, casting many looks behind me. I pursued my way, and, after a longer walk than I had bargained for, reached the high road. At a certain distance below the point at which the long lane I have mentioned entered it, stood a comfortable, tidy dwelling, which might have offered itself as the model of the house which is in no sense haunted—which has no sinister secrets, and knows nothing but blooming prosperity. Its clean white paint stared placidly through the dusk, and its vine-covered porch had been dressed in straw for the winter. An old, one-horse chaise, freighted with two departing visitors was leaving the door, and through the undraped windows, I saw the lamp-lit sitting-room, and the table spread with the early "tea", which had been improvised for the comfort of the guests. The mistress of the house had come to the gate with her friends; she lingered there after the chaise had wheeled creakingly away, half to watch them down the road, and half to give me as I passed in the twilight, a questioning look. She was a comely, quick young woman, with a sharp, dark, eye, and I ventured to stop and speak to her.

"That house down that side-road," I said, "about a mile from here—the only one—can you tell me whom it belongs to?"

She stared at me a moment, and, I thought, coloured a little. "Our folks never go down that road," she said briefly.

"But it's a short way to Medford," I answered.

She gave a little toss of her head. "Perhaps it would turn out a long way. At any rate, we don't use it."

This was interesting. A thrifty Yankee household must have good reasons for this scorn of time-saving processes. "But you know the house, at least?" I said.

"Well, I have seen it."

"And to whom does it belong?"

She gave a little laugh and looked away as if she were aware that, to a stranger, her words might seem to savour of agricultural superstition. "I guess it belongs to them that are in it."

"But is there any one in it? It is completely closed."

"That makes no difference. They never come out, and no one ever goes in." And she turned away.

But I laid my hand on her arm, respectfully. "You mean," I said, "that the house is haunted?"

She drew herself away, coloured, raised her finger to her lips, and hurried into the house, where, in a moment, the curtains were dropped over the windows.

For several days, I thought repeatedly of this little adventure, but I took some satisfaction in keeping it to myself. If the house was not haunted, it was useless to expose my imaginative whims, and if it was, it was agreeable to drain the cup of horror without assistance. I determined, of course, to pass that way again; and a week later—it was the last day of the year—I retraced my steps. I approached the house from the opposite direction, and found myself before it about the same hour as before. The light was failing, the sky low and grey; the wind wailed along the hard, bare ground, and made slow eddies of the frost-blackened leaves. The melancholy mansion stood there, seeming to gather the winter twilight around it, and mask itself in it, inscrutably. I hardly knew on what errand I had come, but I had a vague feeling that if this time the door-knob were to turn and the door to open, I should take my heart in my hands, and let them close behind me. Who were the mysterious tenants to whom the good woman at the corner had alluded? What had been seen or heard—what was related? The door was stubborn as before, and my impertinent fumblings with the latch caused no upper window to be thrown open, nor any strange, pale face to be thrust out. I ventured even to raise the rusty knocker and give it half-a-dozen raps, but they made a flat, dead sound, and aroused no echo. Familiarity breeds contempt; I don't know what I should have done next, if, in the distance, up the road (the same one I had followed), I had not seen a solitary figure advancing. I was unwilling to be observed hanging about this ill-famed dwelling, and I sought refuge among the dense shadows of a grove of pines nearby, where I might peep forth, and yet remain invisible. Presently, the new-comer drew near, and I perceived that he was making straight for the house. He was a little, old man, the most striking feature of whose appearance was a voluminous cloak, of a sort of military cut. He carried a walking-stick, and advanced in a slow, painful, somewhat hobbling fashion, but with an air of extreme resolution. He turned off from the road, and followed the vague wheel-track, and within a few yards of the house he paused. He looked up at it, fixedly and searchingly, as if he were counting the windows, or noting certain familiar marks. Then he took off his hat, and bent over slowly and solemnly, as if he were performing an obeisance. As he stood uncovered, I had a good look at him. He was, as I have said, a diminutive old man, but it would have been hard to decide whether he belonged to this world or to the other. His head reminded me, vaguely, of the portraits of Andrew Jackson. He had a crop of grizzled hair, as stiff as a brush, a lean, pale, smooth-shaven face, and an eye of intense brilliancy, surmounted with thick brows, which had remained perfectly black. His face, as well as his cloak, seemed to belong to an old soldier; he looked like a retired military man of a modest rank; but he struck me as exceeding the classic privilege of even such a personage to be eccentric and grotesque. When he had finished his salute, he advanced to the door, fumbled in the folds of his cloak, which hung down much further in front than behind, and produced a key. This he slowly and carefully inserted into the lock, and then, apparently, he turned it. But the door did not immediately open; first he bent his head, turned his ear, and stood listening, and then he looked up and down the road. Satisfied or reassured, he applied his aged shoulder to one of the deep-set panels, and pressed a moment. The door yielded—opening into perfect darkness. He stopped again on the threshold, and again removed his hat and made his bow. Then he went in, and carefully closed the door behind him.

Who in the world was he, and what was his errand? He might have been a figure out of one of Hoffman's tales. Was he vision or a reality—an inmate of the house, or a familiar, friendly visitor? What had been the meaning, in either case, of his mystic genuflexions, and how did he propose to proceed, in that inner darkness? I emerged from my retirement and observed narrowly, several of the windows. In each of them, at an interval, a ray of light became visible in the chink between the two leaves of the shutters. Evidently, he was lighting up; was he going to give a party—a ghostly revel? My curiosity grew intense, but I was quite at a loss how to satisfy it. For a moment I thought of rapping peremptorily at the door; but I dismissed this idea as unmannerly, and calculated to break the spell, if spell there was. I walked round the house and tried, without violence, to open one of the lower windows. It resisted, but I had better fortune, in a moment, with another. There was a risk, certainly, in the trick I was playing—a risk of being seen from within, or (worse) seeing, myself, something that I should repent of seeing. But curiosity, as I say, had become an inspiration, and the risk was highly agreeable. Through the parting of the shutters I looked into a lighted room—a room lighted by two candles in old brass flambeaux, placed upon the mantel-shelf. It was apparently a sort of back parlour, and it had retained all its furniture. This was of a homely, old-fashioned pattern, and consisted of hair-cloth chairs and sofas, spare mahogany tables, and framed samplers hung upon the walls. But although the room was furnished, it had a strangely uninhabited look; the tables and chairs were in rigid positions, and no small, familiar objects were visible. I could not see everything, and I could only guess at the existence, on my right, of a large folding-door. It was apparently open, and the light of the neighbouring room passed through it. I waited for some time, but the room remained empty. At last I became conscious that a large shadow was projected upon the wall opposite the folding-door—the shadow, evidently, of a figure in the adjoining room. It was tall and grotesque, and seemed to represent a person sitting perfectly motionless, in profile. I thought I recognized the perpendicular bristles and far-arching nose of my little old man. There was a strange fixedness in his posture; he appeared to be seated, and looking intently at something. I watched the shadow a long time, but it never stirred. At last, however, just as my patience began to ebb, it moved slowly, rose to the ceiling, and became indistinct. I don't know what I should have seen next, but by an irresistible impulse, I closed the shutter. Was it delicacy?—was it pusillanimity? I can hardly say. I lingered, nevertheless, near the house, hoping that my friend would reappear. I was not disappointed; for he at last emerged, looking just as when he had gone in, and taking his leave in the same ceremonious fashion. (The lights, I had already observed, had disappeared from the crevice of each of the windows.) He faced about before the door, took off his hat, and made an obsequious bow. As he turned away I had a hundred minds to speak to him, but I let him depart in peace. This, I may say, was pure delicacy;—you will answer, perhaps, that it came too late. It seemed to me that he had a right to resent my observation; though my own right to exercise it (if ghosts were in the question) struck me as equally positive. I continued to watch him as he hobbled softly down the bank, and along the lonely road. Then I musingly retreated in the opposite direction. I was tempted to follow him, at a distance, to see what became of him; but this, too, seemed indelicate; and I confess, moreover, that I felt the inclination to coquet a little, as it were, with my discovery—to pull apart the petals of the flower one by one.

I continued to smell the flower, from time to time, for its oddity of perfume had fascinated me. I passed by the house on the crossroad again, but never encountered the old man in the cloak, or any other wayfarer. It seemed to keep observers at a distance, and I was careful not to gossip about it; one inquirer, I said to myself, may edge his way into the secret, but there is no room for two. At the same time, of course, I would have been thankful for any chance side-light that might fall across the matter—though I could not well see whence it was to come. I hoped to meet the old man in the cloak elsewhere, but as the days passed by without his reappearing, I ceased to expect it. And yet I reflected that he probably lived in that neighbourhood, inasmuch as he had made his pilgrimage to the vacant house on foot. If he had come from a distance, he would have been sure to arrive in some old deep-hooded gig with yellow wheels—a vehicle as venerably grotesque as himself. One day I took a stroll in Mount Auburn cemetery—an institution at that period in its infancy, and full of a sylvan charm which it has now completely forfeited. It contained more maple and birch than willow and cypress, and the sleepers had ample elbow room. It was not a city of the dead, but at the most a village, and a meditative pedestrian might stroll there without too importunate reminder of the grotesque side of our claims to posthumous consideration. I had come out to enjoy the first foretaste of Spring—one of those mild days of late winter, when the torpid earth seems to draw the first long breath that marks the rupture of the spell of sleep. The sun was veiled in haze, and yet warm, and the frost was oozing from its deepest lurking-places. I had been treading for half an hour the winding ways of the cemetery, when suddenly I perceived a familiar figure seated on a bench against a southward-facing evergreen hedge. I call the figure familiar, because I had seen it often in memory and in fancy; in fact, I had beheld it but once. Its back was turned to me, but it wore a voluminous cloak, which there was no mistaking. Here, at last, was my fellow-visitor at the haunted house, and here was my chance, if I wished to approach him! I made a circuit, and came towards him in front. He saw me, at the end of the alley, and sat motionless, with his hands on the head of his stick, watching me from under his black eyebrows as I drew near. At a distance these black eyebrows looked formidable; they were the only thing I saw in his face. But on a closer view I was reassured, simply because I immediately felt that no man could really be as fantastically fierce as this poor old gentleman looked. His face was a kind of caricature of martial truculence. I stopped in front of him, and respectfully asked leave to sit and rest upon his bench. He granted it with a silent gesture, of much dignity, and I placed myself beside him. In this position I was able, covertly, to observe him. He was quite as much an oddity in the morning sunshine, as he had been in the dubious twilight. The lines in his face were as rigid as if they had been hacked out of a block by a clumsy wood-carver. His eyes were flamboyant, his nose terrific, his mouth implacable. And yet, after a while, when he slowly turned and looked at me, fixedly, I perceived that in spite of this portentous mask, he was a very mild old man. I was sure he even would have been glad to smile, but, evidently, his facial muscles were too stiff—they had taken a different fold, once for all. I wondered whether he was demented, but I dismissed the idea; the fixed glitter in his eye was not that of insanity. What his face really expressed was deep and simple sadness; his heart perhaps was broken, but his brain was intact. His dress was shabby but neat, and his old blue cloak had known half a century's brushing.

I hastened to make some observation upon the exceptional softness of the day, and he answered me in a gently, mellow voice, which it was almost startling to hear proceed from such bellicose lips.

"This is a very comfortable place," he presently added.

"I am fond of walking in graveyards," I rejoined deliberately; flattering myself that I had struck a vein that might lead to something.

I was encouraged; he turned and fixed me with his duskily glowing eyes. Then very gravely,—"Walking, yes. Take all your exercise now. Some day you will have to settle down in a graveyard in a fixed position."

"Very true," said I. "But you know that there are some people who are said to take exercise even after that day."

He had been looking at me still; at this he looked away.

"You don't understand?" I said, gently.

He continued to gaze straight before him.

"Some people, you know, walk about after death," I went on.

At last he turned, and looked at me more portentously than ever. "You don't believe that," he said simply.

"How do you know I don't."

"Because you are young and foolish." This was said without acerbity—even kindly; but in the tone of an old man whose consciousness of his own heavy experience made everything else seem light.

"I am certainly young," I answered; "but I don't think that, on the whole, I am foolish. But say I don't believe in ghosts—most people would be on my side."

"Most people are fools!" said the old man.

I let the question rest, and talked of other things. My companion seemed on his guard, he eyed me defiantly, and made brief answers to my remarks; but I nevertheless gathered an impression that our meeting was an agreeable thing to him, and even a social incident of some importance. He was evidently a lonely creature, and his opportunities for gossip were rare. He had had troubles, and they had detached him from the world, and driven him back upon himself; but the social chord in his antiquated soul was not entirely broken, and I was sure he was gratified to find that it could still feebly resound. At last, he began to ask questions himself; he enquired whether I was a student.

"I am a student of divinity," I answered.

"Of divinity?"

"Of theology. I am studying for the ministry."

At this he eyed me with peculiar intensity—after which his gaze wandered away again. "There are certain things you ought to know, then," he said at last.

"I have a great desire for knowledge," I answered. "What things do you mean?"

He looked at me again awhile, but without heeding my question.

"I like your appearance," he said. "You seem to be a sober lad."

"Oh, I am perfectly sober!" I exclaimed—yet departing for a moment from my soberness.

"I think you are fair-minded," he went on.

"I don't any longer strike you as foolish then?" I asked.

"I stick to what I said about people who deny the power of departed spirits to return. They *are* fools!" And he rapped fiercely with his staff on the earth.

I hesitated a moment, and then, abruptly, "You have seen a ghost!" I said.

He appeared not at all startled.

"You are right, sir!" he answered with great dignity. "With me it's not a matter of cold theory—I have not had to pry into old books to learn what to believe. I *know*! With these eyes I have beheld the departed spirit standing before me as near as you are!" And his eyes, as he spoke, certainly looked as if they had rested upon strange things.

I was irresistibly impressed—I was touched with credulity.

"And was it very terrible?" I asked.

"I am an old soldier—I am not afraid!"

"When was it?—where was it?" I asked.

He looked at me mistrustfully, and I saw that I was going too fast.

"Excuse me from going into particulars," he said. "I am not at liberty to speak more fully. I have told you so much, because I cannot bear to hear this subject spoken of lightly. Remember in future, that you have seen a very honest old man who told you—on his honour—that he had seen a ghost!" And he got up, as if he thought he had said enough. Reserve, shyness, pride, the fear of being laughed at, the memory, possibly, of former strokes of sarcasm—all this, on one side, had its weight with him; but I suspected that on the other, his tongue was loosened by the garrulity of old age, the sense of solitude, and the need of sympathy—and perhaps, also, by the friendliness which he had been so good as to express towards myself. Evidently it would be unwise to press him, but I hoped to see him again.

"To give greater weight to my words," he added, "let me mention my name—Captain Diamond, sir. I have seen service."

"I hope I may have the pleasure of meeting you again," I said.

"The same to you, sir!" And brandishing his stick portentously—though with the friendliest intentions—he marched stiffly away.

I asked two or three persons—selected with discretion—whether they knew anything about Captain Diamond, but they were quite unable to enlighten me. At last, suddenly, I smote my forehead, and, dubbing myself a dolt, remembered that I was neglecting a source of information to which I had never applied in vain. The excellent person at whose table I habitually dined, and who dispensed hospitality to students at so much a week, had a sister as good as herself, and of conversational powers more varied. This sister, who was known as Miss Deborah, was an old maid in all the force of the term. She was deformed, and she never went out of the house; she sat all day at the window, between a birdcage and a flowerpot, stitching small linen articles—mysterious bands and frills. She wielded, I was assured, an exquisite needle, and her work was highly prized. In spite of her deformity and her confinement, she had a little, fresh, round face, and an imperturbable serenity of spirit. She had also a very quick little wit of her own, she was extremely observant, and she had a high relish for a friendly chat. Nothing pleased her so much as to have you—especially, I think, if you were a young divinity student—move your chair near her sunny window, and settle yourself for twenty minutes' "talk". "Well, sir," she used always to say, "what is the latest monstrosity in biblical criticism?"—for she used to pretend to be horrified at the rationalistic tendency of the age. But she was an inexorable little philosopher, and I am convinced that she was a keener rationalist than any of us, and that, if she had chosen, she could have propounded questions that would have made the boldest of us wince. Her window commanded the whole town—or rather, the whole country. Knowledge came to her as she sat singing, with her little, cracked voice, in her low rocking chair. She was the first to learn everything, and the last to forget it. She had the town gossip at her fingers' ends, and she knew everything about people she had never seen. When I asked her how she had acquired her learning, she said simply—"Oh, I observe!" "Observe closely enough," she once said, "and it doesn't matter where you are. You may be in a pitch-dark closet. All you want is something to start with; one thing leads to another, and all things are mixed up. Shut me up in a dark closet and I will observe after a while, that some places in it are darker than others. After that (give me time), and I will tell you what the President of the United States is going to have for dinner." Once I paid her a compliment. "Your observation," I said, "is as fine as your needle, and your statements are as true as your stitches."

Of course Miss Deborah had heard of Captain Diamond. He had been much talked about many years before, but he had survived the scandal that attached to his name.

"What was the scandal?" I asked.

"He killed his daughter."

"Killed her?" I cried; "how so?"

"Oh, not with a pistol, or a dagger, or a dose of arsenic! With his tongue. Talk of women's tongues! He cursed her—with some horrible oath—and she died!"

"What had she done?"

"She had received a visit from a young man who loved her, and whom he had forbidden the house."

"The house," I said—"ah yes! The house is out in the country, two or three miles from here, on a lonely crossroad."

Miss Deborah looked sharply at me, as she bit her thread.

"Ah, you know about the house?" she said.

"A little," I answered; "I have seen it. But I want you to tell me more."

But here Miss Deborah betrayed an incommunicativeness which was most unusual.

"You wouldn't call me superstitious, would you?" she asked.

"You?—you are the quintessence of pure reason."

"Well, every thread has its rotten place and every needle its grain of rust. I would rather not talk about that house."

"You have no idea how you excite my curiosity!" I said.

"I can feel for you. But it would make me very nervous."

"What harm can come to you?" I asked.

"Some harm came to a friend of mine." And Miss Deborah gave a very positive nod.

"What had your friend done?"

"She had told me Captain Diamond's secret, which he had told her with a mighty mystery. She had been an old flame of his, and he took her into his confidence. He bade her tell no one, and assured her that if she did, something dreadful would happen to her."

"And what happened to her?"

"She died."

"Oh, we are all mortal!" I said. "Had she given him a promise?"

"She had not taken it seriously, she had not believed him. She repeated the story to me, and three days afterwards, she was taken with inflammation of the lungs. A month afterwards, here where I sit now, I was stitching her grave-clothes. Since then, I have never mentioned what she told me."

"Was it very strange?"

"It was strange, but it was ridiculous too. It is a thing to make you shudder and to make you laugh, both. But you can't worry it out of me. I am sure that if I were to tell you, I should immediately break a needle in my finger, and die the next week of lock-jaw."

I retired, and urged Miss Deborah no further; but every two or three days, after dinner, I came and sat down by her rocking chair. I made no further allusion to Captain Diamond; I sat silent, clipping tape with her scissors. At last, one day, she told me I was looking poorly. I was pale.

"I am dying of curiosity," I said. "I have lost my appetite. I have eaten no dinner."

"Remember Bluebeard's wife!" said Miss Deborah.

"One may as well perish by the sword as by famine!" I answered. Still she said nothing, and at last I rose with a melodramatic sigh and departed. As I reached the door she called me and pointed to the chair I had vacated. "I never was hard-hearted," she said. "Sit down, and if we are to perish, may we at least perish together." And then, in very few words, she communicated what she knew of Captain Diamond's secret. "He was a very high-tempered old man, and though he was very fond of his daughter, his will was law. He had picked out a husband for her, and given her due notice. Her mother was dead, and they lived alone together. The house had been Mrs Diamond's own marriage portion; the Captain, I believe, hadn't a penny. After his marriage they had come to live there, and he had begun to work the farm. The poor girl's lover was a young man with whiskers from Boston. The Captain came in one evening and found them together; he collared the young man, and hurled a terrible curse at the poor girl. The young man cried that she was his wife, and he asked her if it was true. She said, No! Thereupon Captain Diamond, his fury growing fiercer, repeated his imprecation, ordered her out of the house, and disowned her forever. She swooned away, but her father went raging off and left her. Several hours later, he came back and found the house empty. On the table was a note from the young man telling him that he had killed his daughter, repeating the assurance that she was his own wife, and declaring that he himself claimed the sole right to commit her remains to earth. He had carried the body away in a gig! Captain Diamond wrote him a dreadful note in answer, saying that he didn't believe his daughter was dead, but that, whether or no, she was dead to him. A week later, in the middle of the night, he saw her ghost. Then, I suppose, he was convinced. The ghost reappeared several times, and finally began regularly to haunt the house. It made the old man very uncomfortable, for little by little his passion had passed away, and he was given up to grief. He determined at last to leave the place, and tried to sell it or rent it; but meanwhile the story had gone abroad, the ghost had been seen by other persons, the house had a bad name, and it was impossible to dispose of it. With the farm, it was the old man's only property; and his only means of subsistence; if he could neither live in it nor rent it, he was beggared. But the ghost had no mercy, as he had had none. He struggled for six months, and at last he broke down. He put on his old blue cloak and took up his staff, and prepared to wander away and beg his bread. Then the ghost relented, and proposed a compromise. "Leave the house to me!" it said; "I have marked it for my own. Go off and live elsewhere. But to enable you to live, I will be your tenant, since you can find no other. I will hire the house off you and pay you a certain rent." And the ghost named a sum. The old man consented, and he goes every quarter to collect his rent!"

I laughed at this recital, but I confess I shuddered too, for my own observation had exactly confirmed it. Had I not been witness of one of the Captain's quarterly visits, had I not all but seen him sit watching his spectral tenant count out the rent-money, and when he trudged away in the dark, had he not a little bag of strangely gotten coin hidden in the folds of his old blue cloak? I imparted none of these reflections to Miss Deborah, for I was determined that my observations should have a sequel, for I promised myself the pleasure of treating her to my story in its full maturity. "Captain Diamond," I asked, "has no other known means of subsistence?"

"None whatever. He toils not, neither does he spin—his ghost supports him. A haunted house is valuable property!"

"And in what coin does the ghost pay?"

"In good American gold and silver. It has only this peculiarity—that the pieces are all dated before the young girl's death. It's a strange mixture of matter and spirit!"

"And does the ghost do things handsomely; is the rent large?"

"The old man, I believe, lives decently, and has his pipe and his glass. He took a little house down by the river; the door is sidewise to the street, and there is a little garden before it. There he spends his days, and has an old coloured woman to do for him. Some years ago, he used to wander about a good deal, he was a familiar figure in the town, and most people knew his legend. But of late he has drawn back into his shell; he sits over his fire, and curiosity has forgotten him. I suppose he is falling into his dotage. But I am sure, I trust," said Miss Deborah in conclusion, "that he won't outlive his faculties or his powers of locomotion, for, if I remember rightly, it was part of the bargain that he should come in person to collect his rent."

We neither of us seemed likely to suffer any especial penalty for Miss Deborah's indiscretion; I found her, day after day, singing over her work, neither more nor less active than usual. For myself, I boldly pursued my observations. I went again, more than once, to the great graveyard, but I was disappointed in my hope of finding Captain Diamond there. I had a prospect, however, which afforded me compensation. I shrewdly inferred that the old man's quarterly pilgrimages were made upon the last day of the old quarter. My first sight of him had been on the 31st December, and it was probable that he would return to his haunted home on the last day of March. This was near at hand; at last it arrived. I betook myself late in the afternoon to the old house on the crossroad, supposing that the hour of twilight was the appointed season. I was not wrong. I had been hovering about for a short time, feeling very much like a restless ghost myself, when he appeared in the same manner as before, and wearing the same costume. I again concealed myself, and saw him enter the house with the ceremonial which he had used on the former occasion. A light appeared successively in the crevice of each pair of shutters, and I opened the window which had yielded to my importunity before. Again I saw nothing else. The old man reappeared at last, made his fantastic salaam before the house, and crept away into the dusk.

One day, more than a month after this, I met him again at Mount Auburn. The air was full of the voice of Spring; the birds had come back and were twittering over their Winter's travels, and a mild west wind was making a thin murmur in the raw verdure. He was seated on a bench in the sun, still muffled in his enormous mantle, and he recognized me as soon as I approached him. He nodded at me as if he were an old Bashaw giving me the signal for my decapitation, but it was apparent that he was pleased to see me.

"I have looked for you here more than once," I said. "you don't come often."

"What did you want of me?" he asked.

"I wanted to enjoy your conversation. I did so greatly when I met you here before."

"You found me amusing?"

"Interesting!" I said.

"You didn't think me cracked?"

"Cracked?—My dear sir—!" I protested.

"I'm the sanest man in the country. I know that is what insane people always say; but generally they can't prove it. I can!"

"I believe it," I said. "But I am curious to know how such a thing can be proved."

He was silent awhile.

"I will tell you. I once committed, unintentionally, a great crime. Now I pay the penalty. I give up my life to it. I don't shirk it; I face it squarely, knowing perfectly what it is. I haven't tried to bluff it off; I haven't begged off from it; I haven't run away from it. The penalty is terrible, but I have accepted it. I have been a philosopher!

"If I were a Catholic, I might have turned monk, and spent the rest of my life in fasting and praying. That is no penalty; that is an evasion. I might have blown my brains out—I might have gone mad. I wouldn't do either. I would simply face the music, take the consequences. As I say, they are awful! I take them on certain days, four times a year. So it has been these twenty years; so it will be as long as I last. It's my business; it's my vocation. That's the way I feel about it. I call that reasonable!"

"Admirably so!" I said. "But you fill me with curiosity and with compassion."

"Especially with curiosity," he said, cunningly.

"Why," I answered, "if I know exactly what you suffer I can pity you more."

"I'm much obliged. I don't want your pity; it won't help me. I'll tell you something, but it's not for myself; it's for your own sake." He paused a long time and looked all round him, as if for chance eavesdroppers. I anxiously awaited his revelation, but he disappointed me. "Are you still studying theology?" he asked.

"Oh, yes," I answered, perhaps with a shade of irritation. "It's a thing one can't learn in six months."

"I should think not, so long as you have nothing but your books.

Do you know the proverb, 'A grain of experience is worth a pound of precept?' I'm a great theologian."

"Ah, you have had experience," I murmured sympathetically.

"You have read about the immortality of the soul; you have seen Jonathan Edwards and Dr Hopkins chopping logic over it, and deciding, by chapter and verse, that it is true. But I have seen it with these eyes; I have touched it with these hands!" And the old man held up his rugged old fists and shook them portentously; "That's better!" he went on; "but I have bought it dearly. You had better take it from the books—evidently you always will. You are a very good young man; you will never have a crime on your conscience."

I answered with some juvenile fatuity, that I certainly hoped I had my share of human passions, good young man and prospective Doctor of Divinity as I was.

"Ah, but you have a nice, quiet little temper," he said. "So have I—now! But once I was very brutal—very brutal. You ought to know that such things are. I killed my own child."

"Your own child?"

"I struck her down to the earth and left her to die. They could not hang me, for it was not with my hand I struck her. It was with foul and damnable words. That makes a difference; it's a grand law we live under! Well, sir, I can answer for it that *her* soul is immortal. We have an appointment to meet four times and year, and then I catch it!"

"She has never forgiven you?"

"She has forgiven me as the angels forgive! That's what I can't stand—the soft, quiet way she looks at me. I'd rather she twisted a knife about in my heart—O Lord, Lord, Lord!" and Captain Diamond bowed his head over his stick, and leaned his forehead on his crossed hands.

I was impressed and moved, and his attitude seemed for the moment a check to further questions. Before I ventured to ask him anything more, he slowly rose and pulled his old cloak around him. He was unused to talking about his troubles, and his memories overwhelmed him. "I must go my way," he said; "I must be creeping along."

"I shall perhaps meet you here again," I said.

"Oh, I'm a stiff-jointed old fellow," he answered, "and this is rather far for me to come. I have to reserve myself. I have sat sometimes a month at a time smoking my pipe in my chair. But I should like to see you again." And he stopped and looked at me, terribly and kindly. "Some day, perhaps, I shall be glad to be able to lay my hand on a young, unperverted soul. If a man can make a friend, it is always something gained. What is your name?"

I had in my pocket a small volume of Pascal's *Thoughts*, on the flyleaf of which were written my name and address. I took it out and offered it to my old friend. "Pray keep this little book," I said. "It is one I am very fond of, and it will tell you something about me."

He took it and turned it over slowly, then looking up at me with a scowl of gratitude, "I'm not much of a reader," he said; "but I won't refuse the first present I shall have received since—my troubles; and the last. Thank you, sir!" And with the little book in his hand he took his departure.

I was left to imagine him for some weeks after that sitting solitary in his armchair with his pipe. I had not another glimpse of him. But I was awaiting my chance, and on the last day of June, another quarter having elapsed, I deemed that it had come. The evening dusk in June falls late, and I was impatient for its coming. At last, towards the end of a lovely summer's day, I revisited Captain Diamond's property. Everything now was green around it save the blighted orchard in its rear, but its own immitigable greyness and sadness were as striking as when I had first beheld it beneath a December sky. As I drew near it, I saw that I was late for my purpose, for my purpose had simply been to step forward on Captain Diamond's arrival, and bravely ask him to let me go in with him. He had preceded me, and there were lights already in the windows. I was unwilling, of course, to disturb him during his ghostly interview, and I waited till he came forth. The lights disappeared in the course of time; then the door opened and Captain Diamond stole out. That evening he made no bow to the haunted house, for the first object he beheld was his fair-minded young friend planted, modestly but firmly, near the doorstep. He stopped short, looking at me, and this time his terrible scowl was in keeping with the situation.

"I knew you were here," I said. "I came on purpose."

He seemed dismayed, and looked round at the house uneasily.

"I beg your pardon if I have ventured too far," I added, "but you know you have encouraged me."

"How did you know I was here?"

"I reasoned it out. You told me half your story, and I guessed the other half. I am a great observer, and I had noticed this house in passing. It seemed to me to have a mystery. When you kindly confided to me that you saw spirits, I was sure that it could only be here that you saw them."

"You are mighty clever," cried the old man. "And what brought you here this evening?"

I was obliged to evade the question.

"Oh, I often come; I like to look at the house—it fascinates me."

He turned and looked up at it himself. "It's nothing to look at outside." He was evidently quite unaware of its peculiar outward appearance, and this odd fact, communicated to me thus in the twilight, and under the very brow of the sinister dwelling, seemed to make his vision of the strange things within more real.

"I have been hoping," I said, "for a chance to see the inside. I thought I might find you here, and that you would let me go in with you. I should like to see what you see."

He seemed confounded by my boldness, but not altogether displeased. He laid his hand on my arm. "Do you know what I see?" he asked.

"How can I know, except as you said the other day, by experience? I want to have the experience. Pray, open the door and take me in."

Captain Diamond's brilliant eyes expanded beneath their dusky brows, and after holding his breath a moment, he indulged in the first and last apology for a laugh by which I was to see his solemn visage contorted. It was profoundly grotesque, but it was perfectly noiseless. "Take you in?" he softly growled. "I wouldn't go in again before my time's up for a thousand times that sum." And he thrust out his hand from the folds of his cloak and exhibited a small agglomeration of coin, knotted into the corner of an old silk pocket-handkerchief. "I stick to my bargain no less, but no more!"

"But you told me the first time I had the pleasure of talking with you that it was not so terrible."

"I don't say it's terrible—now. But it's damned disagreeable!"

This adjective was uttered with a force that made me hesitate and reflect. While I did so, I thought I heard a slight movement of one of the window-shutters above us. I looked up, but everything seemed motionless. Captain Diamond, too, had been thinking; suddenly he turned towards the house. "If you will go in alone," he said, "you are welcome."

"Will you wait for me here?"

"Yes, you will not stop long."

"But the house is pitch dark. When you go you have lights."

He thrust his hand into the depths of his cloak and produced some matches. "Take these," he said. "You will find two candlesticks with candles on the table in the hall. Light them, take one in each hand and go ahead."

"Where shall I go?"

"Anywhere—everywhere. You can trust the ghost to find you."

I will not pretend to deny that by this time my heart was beating. And yet I imagine I motioned the old man with a sufficiently dignified gesture to open the door. I had made up my mind that there was in fact a ghost. I had conceded the premise. Only I had assured myself that once the mind was prepared, and the thing was not a surprise, it was possible to keep cool. Captain Diamond turned the lock, flung back the door, and bowed low to me as I passed in. I stood in the darkness, and heard the door close behind me. For some moments, I stirred neither finger nor toe; I stared bravely into the impenetrable dusk. But I saw nothing and heard nothing, and at last I struck a match. On the table were two brass candlesticks rusty from disuse. I lighted the candles and began my tour of exploration.

A wide staircase rose in front of me, guarded by an antique balustrade of that rigidly delicate carving which is found so often in old New England houses. I postponed ascending it, and turned in the room on my right. This was an old-fashioned parlour meagrely furnished, and musty with the absence of human life. I raised my two lights aloft and saw nothing but its empty chairs and its blank walls. Behind me was the room into which I had peeped from without, and which, in fact, communicated with it, as I had supposed, by folding doors. Here, too, I found myself confronted by no menacing spectre. I crossed the hall again, and visited the rooms on the other side; a dining-room in front, where I might have written my name with my finger in the deep dust of the great square table; a kitchen behind with its pots and pans eternally cold. All this was hard and grim, but it was not formidable. I came back into the hall, and walked to the foot of the staircase, holding up my candles; to ascend required a fresh effort, and I was scanning the gloom above. Suddenly, with an inexpressible sensation, I became aware that this gloom was animated; it seemed to move and gather itself together. Slowly—I say slowly, for to my tense expectancy the instants appeared ages—it took the shape of a large, definite figure, and this figure advanced and stood at the top of the stairs. I frankly confess that by this time I was conscious of a feeling to which I am in duty bound to apply the vulgar name of fear. I may poetize it and call it Dread, with a capital letter; it was at any rate the feeling that makes a man yield ground. I measured it as it grew, and it seemed perfectly irresistible; for it did not appear to come from within but without, and to be embodied in the dark image at the head of the staircase. After a fashion I reasoned—I remember reasoning. I said to myself, "I had always thought ghosts were white and transparent; this is a thing of thick shadows, densely opaque." I reminded myself that the occasion was momentous, and that if fear were to overcome me I should gather all possible impressions while my wits remained. I stepped back, foot behind foot, with my eyes still on the figure and placed my candles on the table. I was perfectly conscious that the proper thing was to ascend the stairs resolutely, face to face with the image, but the soles of my shoes seemed suddenly to have been transformed into leaden weights. I had got what I wanted; I was seeing the ghost. I tried to look at the figure distinctly so that I could remember it, and fairly claim, afterwards, not to have lost my self-possession. I even asked myself how long it was expected I should stand looking, and how soon I could honourably retire. All this, of course, passed through my mind with extreme rapidity, and it was checked by a further movement on the part of the figure. Two white hands appeared in the dark perpendicular mass, and were slowly raised to what seemed to be the level of the head. Here they were pressed together, over the region of the face, and then they were removed, and the face was disclosed. It was dim, white, strange, in every way ghostly. It looked down at me for an instant, after which one of the hands was raised again, slowly, and waved to and fro before it. There was something very singular in this gesture; it seemed to denote resentment and dismissal, and yet it had a sort of trivial, familiar motion. Familiarity on the part of the haunting Presence had not entered into my calculation, and did not strike me pleasantly. I agreed with Captain Diamond that it was "damned disagreeable." I was pervaded by an intense desire to make an orderly, and, if possible, a graceful retreat. I wished to do it gallantly, and it seemed to me that it would be gallant to blow out my candles. I turned and did so, punctiliously, and then I made my way to the door, groped a moment and opened it. The outer light, almost extinct as it was, entered a moment, played over the dusty depths of the house and showed me the solid shadow.

Standing on the grass bent over his stick, under the early glimmering stars, I found Captain Diamond. He looked up at me fixedly for a moment, but asked no questions, and then he went and locked the door. This duty performed, he discharged the other—made his obeisance like the priest before the altar—and then without heeding me further, took his departure.

A few days later, I suspended my studies and went off for the summer's vacation. I was absent for several weeks, during which I had plenty of leisure to analyse my impressions of the supernatural. I took some satisfaction in the reflection that I had not been ignobly terrified; I had not bolted nor swooned—I had proceeded with dignity. Nevertheless, I was certainly more comfortable when I had put thirty miles between me and the scene of my exploit, and I continued for many days to prefer the daylight to the dark. My nerves had been powerfully excited; of this I was particularly conscious when, under the influence of the drowsy air of the seaside, my excitement began slowly to ebb. As it disappeared, I attempted to take a sternly rational view of my experience. Certainly I had seen *something*—that was not fancy; but what had I seen? I regretted extremely now that I had not been bolder, that I had not gone nearer and inspected the apparition more minutely. But it was very well to talk; I had done as much as any man in the circumstances would have dared; it was indeed a physical impossibility that I should have advanced. Was not this paralysis of my powers in itself a supernatural influence? Not necessarily, perhaps, for a sham ghost that one accepted might do as much execution as a real ghost. But why had I so easily accepted the sable phantom that waved its hand? Why had it so impressed itself? Unquestionably, true or false, it was a very clever phantom. I greatly preferred that it should have been true—in the first place because I did not care to have shivered and shaken for nothing, and in the second place because to have seen a well-authenticated goblin is, as things go, a feather in a quiet man's cap. I tried, therefore, to let my vision rest and to stop turning it over. But an impulse stronger than my will recurred at intervals and set a mocking question on my lips. Granted that the apparition was Captain Diamond's daughter; if it was she it certainly was her spirit. But was it not her spirit and something more?

The middle of September saw me again established among the theologic shades, but I made no haste to revisit the haunted house.

The last of the month approached—the term of another quarter with poor Captain Diamond—and found me indisposed to disturb his pilgrimage on this occasion; though I confess that I thought with a good deal of compassion of the feeble old man trudging away, lonely, in the autumn dusk, on his extraordinary errand. On the thirtieth of September, at noonday, I was drowsing over a heavy octavo, when I heard a feeble rap at my door. I replied with an invitation to enter, but as this produced no effect I repaired to the door and opened it. Before me stood an elderly negress with her head bound in a scarlet turban, and a white handkerchief folded across her bosom. She looked at me intently and in silence; she had that air of supreme gravity and decency which aged persons of her race so often wear. I stood interrogative, and at last, drawing her hand from her ample pocket, she held up a little book. It was the copy of Pascal's *Thoughts* that I had given to Captain Diamond.

"Please, sir," she said, very mildly, "do you know this book?"

"Perfectly," said I, "my name is on the flyleaf."

"It is your name—no other?"

"I will write my name if you like, and you can compare them," I answered.

She was silent a moment and then, with dignity—"It would be useless, sir," she said, "I can't read. If you will give me your word that is enough. I come," she went on, "from the gentleman to whom you gave the book. He told me to carry it as a token—a token—that is what he called it. He is right down sick, and he wants to see you."

"Captain Diamond—sick?" I cried. "Is his illness serious?"

"He is very bad—he is all gone."

I expressed my regret and sympathy, and offered to go to him immediately, if his sable messenger would show me the way. She assented deferentially, and in a few moments I was following her along the sunny streets, feeling very much like a personage in the Arabian Nights, led to a postern gate by an Ethiopian slave. My own conductress directed her steps towards the river and stopped at a decent little yellow house in one of the streets that descend to it. She quickly opened the door and led me in, and I very soon found myself in the presence of my old friend. He was in bed, in a darkened room, and evidently in a very feeble state. He lay back on his pillow staring before him, with his bristling hair more erect than ever, and his intensely dark and bright old eyes touched with the glitter of fever. His apartment was humble and scrupulously neat and I could see that my dusky guide was a faithful servant. Captain Diamond, lying there rigid and pale on his white sheets, resembled some ruggedly carven figure on the lid of a Gothic tomb. He looked at me silently, and my companion withdrew and left us alone.

"Yes, it's you," he said, at last, "it's you, that good young man. There is no mistake, is there?"

"I hope not; I believe I'm a good young man. But I am very sorry you are ill. What can I do for you?"

"I am very bad, very bad; my poor old bones ache so!" and, groaning portentously, he tried to turn towards me.

I questioned him about the nature of his malady and the length of time he had been in bed, but he barely heeded me; he seemed impatient to speak of something else. He grasped my sleeve, pulled me towards him and whispered quickly:

"You know my time's up!"

"Oh, I trust not," I said, mistaking his meaning. "I shall certainly see you on your legs again."

"God knows!" he cried. "But I don't mean I'm dying; not yet a bit. What I mean is, I'm due at the house. This is rent-day."

"Oh, exactly! But you can't go."

"I can't go. It's awful. I shall lose my money. If I am dying, I want it all the same. I want to pay the doctor. I want to be buried like a respectable man."

"Is it this evening?" I asked.

"This evening at sunset, sharp."

He lay staring at me, and, as I looked at him in return, I suddenly understood his motive for sending for me. Morally, as it came into my thought, I winced. But, I suppose I looked unperturbed, for he continued in the same tone. "I can't lose my money. Some one else must go. I asked Belinda; but she won't hear of it."

"You believe the money will be paid to another person?"

"We can try, at least. I have never failed before and I don't know. But, if you say I'm as sick as a dog, that my old bones ache, that I'm dying, perhaps she'll trust you. She don't want me to starve!"

"You would like me to go in your place, then?"

"You have been there once; you know what it is. Are you afraid?"

I hesitated.

"Give me three minutes to reflect," I said, "and I will tell you." My glance wandered over the room and rested on the various objects that spoke of the threadbare, decent poverty of its occupant. There seemed to be a mute appeal to my pity and my resolution in their cracked and faded sparseness. Meanwhile Captain Diamond continued, feebly:

"I think she'd trust you, as I have trusted you; she'll like your face; she'll see there is no harm in you. It's a hundred and thirty-three dollars, exactly. Be sure you put them into a safe place."

"Yes," I said at last, "I will go, and, so far as it depends upon me, you shall have the money by nine o'clock tonight."

He seemed greatly relieved; he took my hand and faintly pressed it, and soon afterwards I withdrew. I tried for the rest of the day not to think of my evening's work, but, of course, I thought of nothing else. I will not deny that I was nervous; I was, in fact, greatly excited, and I spent my time in alternately hoping that the mystery should prove less deep than it appeared, and yet fearing that it might prove too shallow. The hours passed very slowly, but, as the afternoon began to wane, I started on my mission. On the way, I stopped at Captain Diamond's modest dwelling, to ask how he was doing, and to receive such last instructions as he might desire to lay upon me. The old negress, gravely and inscrutably placid, admitted me, and, in answer to my enquiries, said that the Captain was very low; he had sunk since the morning.

"You must be right smart," she said, "if you want to get back before he drops off."

A glance assured me that she knew of my projected expedition, though, in her own opaque black pupil, there was not a gleam of self-betrayal.

"But why should Captain Diamond drop off?" I asked. "He certainly seems very weak; but I cannot make out that he has any definite disease."

"His disease is old age," she said, sententiously.

"But he is not so old as that; sixty-seven or sixty-eight, at most."

She was silent a moment.

"He's worn out; he's used up; he can't stand it any longer."

"Can I see him a moment?" I asked; upon which she led me again to his room.

He was lying in the same way as when I had left him, except that his eyes were closed. But he seemed very "low", as she had said, and he had very little pulse. Nevertheless, I further learned the doctor had been there in the afternoon and professed himself satisfied. "He don't know what's been going on," said Belinda, curtly.

The old man stirred a little, opened his eyes, and after some time recognized me.

"I'm going, you know," I said. "I'm going for your money. Have you anything more to say?" He raised himself slowly, and with a painful effort, against his pillows; but he seemed hardly to understand me. "The house, you know," I said. "Your daughter."

He rubbed his forehead, slowly, awhile, and at last, his comprehension awoke. "Ah, yes," he murmured, "I trust you. A hundred and thirty-three dollars. In old pieces—all in old pieces." Then he added more vigorously, and with a brightening eye: "Be very respectful—be very polite. If not—if not—" and his voice failed again.

"Oh, I certainly shall be," I said, with a rather forced smile. "But, if not?"

"If not, I shall know it!" he said, very gravely. And with this, his eyes closed and he sunk down again.

I took my departure and pursued my journey with a sufficiently resolute step. When I reached the house, I made a propitiatory bow in front of it, in emulation of Captain Diamond. I had timed my walk to as to be able to enter without delay; night had already fallen. I turned the key, opened the door and shut it behind me. Then I struck a light, and found the two candlesticks I had used before, standing on the tables in the entry. I applied a match to both of them, took them up and went into the parlour. It was empty, and though I waited awhile, it remained empty. I passed then into the other rooms on the same floor, and no dark image rose before me to check my steps. At last, I came out into the hall again, and stood weighing the question of going upstairs. The staircase had been the scene of my discomfiture before, and I approached it with profound mistrust. At the foot, I paused, looking up, with my hand on the balustrade. I was acutely expectant, and my expectation was justified. Slowly, in the darkness above, the black figure that I had seen before took shape. It was not an illusion; it was a figure, and the same. I gave it time to define itself, and watched it stand and look down at me with its hidden face. Then deliberately, I lifted my voice and spoke.

"I have come in place of Captain Diamond, at his request," I said. "He is very ill; he is unable to leave his bed. He earnestly begs that you will pay the money to me; I will immediately carry it to him." The figure stood motionless, giving no sign. "Captain Diamond would have come if he were able to move." I added, in a moment, appealingly; "but, he is utterly unable."

At this the figure slowly unveiled its face and showed me a dim, white mask; then it began slowly to descend the stairs. Instinctively I fell back before it, retreating to the door of the front sitting-room. With my eyes still fixed on it, I moved backward across the threshold; then I stopped in the middle of the room and set down my lights. The figure advanced; it seemed to be that of a tall woman, dressed in vaporous black crape. As it drew near, I saw that it had a perfectly human face, though it looked extremely pale and sad. We stood gazing at each other; my agitation had completely vanished; I was only deeply interested.

"Is my father dangerously ill?" said the apparition.

At the sound of its voice—gentle, tremulous, and perfectly human—I started forward; I felt a rebound of excitement. I drew a long breath, I gave a sort of cry, for what I saw before me was not a disembodied spirit, but a beautiful women, an audacious actress. Instinctively, irresistibly, by the force of reaction against my credulity, I stretched out my hand and seized the long veil that muffled her head. I gave it a violent jerk, dragged it nearly off, and stood staring at a large fair person, of about five-and-thirty. I comprehended her at a glance; her long black dress, her pale, sorrow-worn face, painted to look paler, her very fine eyes—the colour of her father's—and her sense of outrage at my movement.

"My father, I suppose," she cried, "did not send you here to insult me!" and she turned away rapidly, took up one of the candles and moved towards the door. Here she paused, looked at me again, hesitated, and then drew a purse from her pocked and flung it down on the floor. "There is your money!" she said majestically.

I stood there, wavering between amazement and shame, and saw her pass out into the hall. Then I picked up the purse. The next moment, I heard a loud shriek and a crash of something dropping, and she came staggering back into the room without her light.

"My father—my father!" she cried; and with parted lips and dilated eyes, she rushed towards me.

"Your father—where?" I demanded.

"In the hall, at the foot of the stairs."

I stepped forward to go out, but she seized my arm.

"He is in white," she cried, "in his shirt. It's not he!"

"Why, your father is in his house, in his bed, extremely ill," I answered.

She looked at me fixedly, with searching eyes.

"Dying?"

"I hope not," I stuttered.

She gave a long moan and covered her face with her hands.

"Oh, heavens, I have seen his ghost!" she cried.

She still held my arm; she seemed too terrified to release it. "His ghost!" I echoed, wondering.

"It's the punishment of my long folly!" she went on.

"Ah," said I, "it's the punishment of my indiscretion—of my violence!"

"Take me away, take me away!" she cried, still clinging to my arm. "Not there"—as I was turning towards the hall and the front door—"not there, for pity's sake! By this door—the back entrance." And snatching the other candle from the table, she led me through the neighbouring room into the back part of the house. Here was a door opening from a sort of scullery into the orchard. I turned the rusty lock and we passed out and stood in the cool air, beneath the stars. Here my companion gathered her black drapery about her, and stood for a moment, hesitating. I had been infinitely flurried, but my curiosity touching her was uppermost. Agitated, pale, picturesque, she looked, in the early evening light, very beautiful.

"You have been playing all these years a most extraordinary game," I said.

She looked at me sombrely, and seemed disinclined to reply. "I came in perfect good faith," I went on. "The last time—three months ago—you remember?—you greatly frightened me."

"Of course it was an extraordinary game," she answered at last. "But it was the only way."

"Had he not forgiven you?"

"So long as he thought me dead, yes. There have been things in my life he could not forgive."

I hesitated and then—"And where is your husband?" I asked.

"I have no husband—I have never had a husband."

She made a gesture which checked further questions, and moved rapidly away. I walked with her round the house to the road, and she kept murmuring—"It was he—it was he!" When we reached the road she stopped, and asked me which way I was going. I pointed to the road by which I had come, and she said—"I take the other. You are going to my father's?" she added.

"Directly," I said.

"Will you let me know tomorrow what you have found?"

"With pleasure. But how shall I communicate with you?"

She seemed at a loss, and looked about her. "Write a few words," she said, "and put them under that stone." And she pointed to one of the lava slabs that bordered the old well. I gave her my promise to comply, and she turned away. "I know my road," she said. "Everything is arranged. It's an old story."

She left me with a rapid step, and as she receded into the darkness, resumed, with the dark flowing lines of her drapery, the phantasmal appearance with which she had at first appeared to me. I watched her till she became invisible, and then I took my own leave of the place. I returned to town at a swinging pace, and marched straight to the little yellow house near the river. I took the liberty of entering without a knock, and, encountering no interruption, made my way to Captain Diamond's room. Outside the door, on a low bench, with folded arms, sat the sable Belinda.

"How is he?" I asked.

"He's gone to glory."

"Dead?" I cried.

She rose with a sort of tragic chuckle.

"He's as big a ghost as any of them now!"

I passed into the room and found the old man lying there irredeemably rigid and still. I wrote that evening a few lines which I proposed on the morrow to place beneath the stone, near the well; but my promise was not destined to be executed. I slept that night very ill—it was natural—and in my restlessness left my bed to walk about the room. As I did so I caught sight, in passing my window, of a red glow in the north-western sky. A house was on fire in the country, and evidently burning fast. It lay in the same direction as the scene of my evening's adventures, and as I stood watching the crimson horizon I was startled by a sharp memory. I had blown out the candle which lighted me, with my companion, to the door through which we escaped, but I had not accounted for the other light, which she had carried into the hall and dropped—heaven knew where—in her consternation. The next day I walked out with my folded letter and turned into the familiar crossroad. The haunted house was a mass of charred beams and smouldering ashes; the well-cover had been pulled off, in quest of water, by the few neighbours who had had the audacity to contest what they must have regarded as a demon-kindled blaze, the loose stones were completely displaced, and the earth had been trampled into puddles.